CAVE OF DEPARTURE

Best Wishes—
Niki Tate

BOOK I
The Estorian Chronicles

CAVE of DEPARTURE

Nikki Tate

Sono
Nis
Press
VICTORIA, BRITISH COLUMBIA

NATIONAL LIBRARY OF CANADA CATALOGUING IN PUBLICATION DATA
Tate, Nikki, 1962-
  Cave of departure

  (The Estorian chronicles trilogy)
  ISBN 1-55039-119-4

  I. Title.
PS8589.A8735C38 2001   jC813'.54 C2001-911139-8
PZ7.T2113Ca 2001

Sono Nis Press gratefully acknowledges the support of the Canada Council for
the Arts and the Province of British Columbia, through the British Columbia
Arts Council.

Edited by Freda Nobbs and Dawn Loewen
Cover and book design by Jim Brennan
Map by E. Colin Williams

Published by
Sono Nis Press
PO Box 5550, Stn. B
Victoria, BC V8R 6S4
1-800-370-5228
sononis@islandnet.com
www.islandnet.com/sononis/

Distributed in the U.S. by
Orca Book Publishers
Box 468
Custer, WA 98240-0468
1-800-210-5277

Printed and bound in Canada.

The Canada Council | Le Conseil des Arts
for the Arts | du Canada

For Aly
May all your stories have happy endings.

ACKNOWLEDGEMENTS

Dominique has always been a bit of a problem child and without the help of many he would never have made it this far. Thanks to Freda and Dawn for your marvelous insights and invaluable editorial input. Jim, your vision of the world Dominique inhabits is amazing—thank you for giving the Island of Tanga such a vivid virtual form. Colin, you did a wonderful job with the map and gave me some excellent input on early drafts—ta. Chris, thank you—you know why. A special thanks to Diane Morriss of Sono Nis Press whose steadfast support and encouragement enabled me to set off on this journey into unknown territory. Last, but certainly not least, a huge thank you to Dani, whose good humour and fine companionship help make those dreadful periods of revisions a little more tolerable.

THE NAMING CEREMONY

"Oh, Mighty Powers, we welcome this child!"

The women passed the Naming basket containing the tiny baby around the circle as Protector Bertolescu chanted,

> *Grand Tellers!*
> *Speak wisely to this boy child!*
> *Share your great knowledge with this infant,*
>   *future of our people.*
> *For when he speaks your Stories, we will*
>   *listen, listen.*

The baby moved from embrace to embrace until, finally, he was returned to his mother. Dania Elnedo lifted her child from the willow basket and welcomed her infant son back with a cuddle and a smile.

"In the name of the Beginning, this boy's name shall be . . ." The clan leader raised his face to the sky and waited.

The tiny boy opened his soft, grey eyes and gazed up at his mother's face. He studied the strong curve of her chin, the lines spreading from the corners of her eyes, the soft texture of her smooth, brown skin. Red and black beads at the ends of hundreds of tight braids clicked as Dania lowered her head towards her baby.

Protector Bertolescu coughed. "And so his name shall be?"

"Dominique. He shall be named Dominique Elnedo, sir."

The Protector nodded his great, shaggy head and said, "And so, we the humble people offer this boy's name to you, Great Keepers of Stories. May he be known to all as Dominique Elnedo, one of the Estorian people, member of the clan of Bertolescu, and future teller of your Stories."

The women sighed and swayed, rocking slowly from side to side, shoulders touching, tears streaking their cheeks. Finally, a boy child for Dania, who had, so far, mothered only girls.

Dania smiled down at the baby in her arms. Now sound asleep, snuggled close against his mother's chest, Dominique was oblivious to the excitement of the Naming Ceremony.

"The stone, Dania?"

Dania nodded. With the broad pad of her thumb she gently wiped the moisture of her own spilled tears from the boy's cheek. She shifted her bundle carefully and pulled an oblong stone from a pouch that hung around her neck.

Dania passed the reddish-brown stone, polished

until it glowed, to the woman on her left. Her sister Panna pressed the stone to her lips and then, with a swift, powerful slash, she struck it with another piece of rock concealed in her hand.

"Welcome, Dominique. I mark you so."

"Dominique. Dominique," the other women chanted.

Panna passed the stone to her left, to Crona, who lifted it to her lips, and then, with a shaking hand, hit it with her own striking rock.

"Welcome, Dominique. I mark you so." Her old voice cracked and she drew her shawl around her hunched shoulders.

"Dominique. Dominique," answered the chorus.

As each woman struck Dominique's stone, her mark was added until the stone had travelled all the way around the circle and returned to Dania. She raised it to her lips and then slipped the mottled and scarred stone into a soft leather pouch hanging around the sleeping baby's neck. She looked up quickly to see whether Protector Bertolescu had noticed how her hand trembled. He had, though he said nothing. But old Crona could not resist.

"So, there will be no mark from the boy's father?" she asked, her crooked fingers tugging at the edge of her shawl.

Dania's eyes flicked from Crona's lined face to Bertolescu's and back. The leader cleared his throat and spoke. "It's not always necessary, Crona, as you well know. Boris Elnedo can choose the time he marks his son's stone. Perhaps when he next returns."

"*If* he returns," the old woman said with a sniff.

Her lips set in a hard line across her face and she looked up pointedly at the wide blue sky as if she herself might hear a message from the Keepers of Stories.

Bertolescu cleared his throat and nodded at Dania, who gently pressed her fingertip to the pouch and the Namingstone it contained.

"And so the boy is named by his people. May he hear the Stories and tell the Stories well!"

With that, Protector Bertolescu raised his arms and all the women but Crona shouted and laughed. Without speaking to the others, Crona collected the sacred Naming basket and wrapped it carefully in its soft woollen travelling blanket. Dania tucked Dominique into the folds of the baby sling she wore across her chest and stomach. The baby nuzzled close without waking up.

"Come, Dania," Panna said. "Bring the baby, Dominique."

"Dominique," Dania repeated, feeling the weight of the new name on her tongue.

"Come, sister. His cousins want to meet him. We move on tomorrow. We will have no time then." More softly Panna added, "Don't worry about old Crona. She will come around. No heart can stay cold against such a beautiful baby."

Dania peeped at her sleeping child and smiled. Her own heart full, she followed the other women back to the encampment.

1

THE SEVENTH YEAR OF SILENCE

*Finally, after the great fire, the boy child,
Enton, left his mother's house.*

"Dania?"

Panna followed her sister to the slow-moving river. At the height of summer, the River Rolenum on the big island of Tanga was thick and sluggish. During the spring runoffs, the water tumbled and roared along, licking hungrily at the grasses growing atop the banks. Now, though, the women of the clan had to scramble right down the muddy banks and wade way out into the gentle current to fill their water pots.

"Dania! Don't ignore me!"

Dominique ran ahead and splashed into the shallows.

"Dominique!" Dania called. "Don't play in there. Fill your water pot quickly. We have work to do."

"Dania, listen to me."

"Not now, Panna. Can you not see we are busy?"

"When, then? You must speak of it."

Dominique dabbled at the water's edge, wiggling his toes into the soft, brown mud.

"Dominique! Do you hear me? Stop playing."

Dominique frowned. It was so predictable. Whenever Panna began her nagging, Mama's good humour vanished.

"Has it happened yet?"

Dania scowled at her sister.

"You know the other boys his age have started. Every one of them. He's the only one, Dania."

"Shh. Not now."

"No. I will not be quiet. You don't want to see it, but there is something wrong with him. Have you consulted with the Protector?"

Dominique lifted his pot and poured the water out in a slow dribble. Usually the musical *plip-plop* of water falling into water delighted him. Today it seemed irritating. He stopped.

"Can he even speak?"

Aunt Panna's questions were so silly. Of course he could speak.

With an angry jerk, Dania tossed her hair back over her shoulder. "You know very well he can talk."

"About what, though? Grinding peska roots? Fetching water? Tormenting his sisters?"

That brought a smile to his face. Dominique crouched down in the water. It wouldn't do for his aunt to see him grinning at the thought of teasing his sisters. Such a flock of galla birds they were! They deserved his tricks.

"And Crona told me Boris refused to add his mark to the Namingstone."

Dominique's mother stiffened and the boy stood up, oblivious to the water trickling down his legs.

"He didn't refuse. He . . . he . . . he forgot."

"Forgot? *Forgot?* A man does not forget to add his mark to his son's stone."

"He does if he rushes into camp in the middle of the night full of talk of conspiracies and kidnappings . . . war and invasions. . . ."

"He had no right to speak of such things with you. Crona says—"

"Stop! I don't want to know any more of what Crona says!"

Dania jerked her bucket from the river so hard, most of the water spilled onto the muddy bank and oozed away.

"Then listen to what I have to say. Your boy is not growing up properly."

Dominique knew his aunt's comments had nothing to do with his size. Any moment now she would start with the Stories from Beyond.

He crouched back down and pulled several stiff chellabong reeds from where they grew at the water's edge.

"Did you know Chenta's boy, Feltham, heard a Story from the Tellers Beyond about a snake?"

"More gossip, sister. Do you not see the trouble you cause?"

"Gossip? Trouble? Not at all. The other boys are

playing around here somewhere. I'll call Feltham."

"No! That's—"

"Feltham!"

Dominique looked up from the cluster of reeds in his hands. Calling Feltham over was a different tactic for his aunt.

"Feltham Tomonok!" Panna's fists rode her hips and her bottom lip pushed out. She turned back to Dania. "Your boy is six. He should be playing with the other boys, not fetching water like a . . . like a girl."

Panna took a deep breath and yelled again. "Feltham!" She puffed out her cheeks and glared at Dominique. "If you spent more time with the boys, maybe you would learn to hear the Stories, too. You should be in a lesson group by now. In all of Western Chanmari there is no such thing as an Estorian boy who does not tell Stories," she chided.

Dominique scowled at the water, careful not to let his aunt see his face. The old wimple-hog could be swallowed by the Sea Caves of Krokoska and he wouldn't miss her.

"Ah, where is that Feltham? Feltham! Come here!"

An answering shout rose from farther along the river.

"What?"

"Come here!"

When Feltham, tall and skinny with a shock of red hair spraying over his forehead, galumphed over the bank, Panna straightened up and pointed first at Dania and then at Dominique.

"You two, listen." She nodded at Feltham. "Go ahead. The snake. Tell them how it happened."

Feltham grinned slyly at Dominique, who let the reeds fall into the river and watched them drift slowly away. Today was not a day for building a little raft.

"I was climbing a tree, over there by the fish traps, when I had to stop."

"What do you mean, you had to stop?" Panna prompted.

"You know, to listen."

"You heard something, then?"

The boy nodded. "Inside. Like a voice, but not quite like a voice." Feltham looked away from Dominique and turned to Panna. When she nodded, he went on.

"And then in my head I saw this snake and the snake had big fangs and came up out of a hole in the ground and told all the people to run away if they wanted to be safe. The snake had red dots over its eyes and . . ." He paused for effect. "And the snake wore a mask made of blue and red beads. Some of the people caught the snake in a basket and when they checked to see if the snake was hungry, it spit strings of blood at them. The blood strings were all sticky and tied them up so the people couldn't breathe. So they died."

The boy stopped. "That's all—for that Story. I have others. I hear them all the time now."

"Thank you, Feltham. The snake Story is enough. Go on now, back to what you were doing."

When Feltham had disappeared back over the riverbank, Dania and Dominique waited for Panna to speak again.

"You see. They are all doing it. Have you ever heard of a snake like that? Wearing a bead mask? Spitting strings of blood? Tying the people up? Feltham is particularly good, but all the boys of Dominique's birth year have started hearing new Stories. What about Dominique?"

"He is very good at telling the Tara stories."

Dominique wished his mother hadn't said anything.

"The Tara stories? Oh, Dania, please!"

"They are stories! Good stories! He is practising. . . ."

"They are women's stories! Nothing more. They are not new. They are not the Stories of men and boys. Don't be stupid."

"I'm not stupid!"

Why couldn't Panna leave him alone? There were plenty of other things to worry about, like how much fish the women were catching or the deep cough in old Granny Poona's chest. Why did she always have to fret about the stupid Stories? Dominique clenched his fists and interrupted the women's squabble.

"Mama!"

"Fill your bucket and go back to the fire."

Dominique flinched, unused to such sharpness. He dipped his bucket into the water, but slowly. He didn't want to hear any more of the fight but he didn't want to miss anything, either.

"You are hiding from the truth, Dania. And if you don't do something about it, then I will talk to Protector Bertolescu myself."

"No." Dania's voice was quiet, but both Dominique and Panna stood absolutely still. "No," said Dania. "I will do what is necessary. Dominique will learn to hear the Stories meant for men. You will see."

Dominique grunted as he lifted his heavy bucket and started to walk back up to the cooking fire. It was the last time he would ever carry water for his mother.

2

TRAVEL ON?
OR BIDE OUR TIME?

*And when, on the seventh night of the siege,
King Krokoska ordered the drawbridge to be
lowered, the king strode forth and the enemy
soldiers fell beneath his mighty blows.*

"Now, hold the image of the warrior king Krokoska
in your minds. . . ."

Dominique closed his eyes as Uncle Sethka
spoke of the great King Krokoska. The easiest thing
to imagine was the king's broad shoulders, wide
enough to carry the great timbers used to build his
mountain fortress, Castle Karnerra.

"What was the colour of his hair?" Sethka asked
the boys.

"Red as the sinking sun as it drops into the Sea
of Perfidium," Pickalotto answered.

"Excellent, son." Uncle Sethka grinned and ruffled his fingers through Pickalotto's hair.

Dominique spat on the ground. If his own father were around he wouldn't be stuck with Uncle Sethka as his teacher, wouldn't have to watch as old Sethka slapped his own sons on the back, beamed with pride whenever they mastered a new lesson. Dominique spat again, watching the spittle turn the patch of dirt dark brown.

"Dominique!"

"Yes, Uncle."

"Would King Krokoska have spit?"

Feltham and Kem nudged each other and laughed.

"No, sir."

"Then kindly refrain from doing so yourself."

"Yes, sir."

Dominique ducked his head to avoid looking at the other boys.

"Boys! Enough. What else do we know about King Krokoska's appearance?"

"Eyes blue as sapphires," offered Kem.

"A forehead high and strong as the jagged peaks of the Krokoska Mountains," said Rotiko, Sethka's second-youngest son. Rotiko was actually a bit younger than the other boys, but was so quick and clever the Protector had granted him special permission to join Sethka's lesson group. Aleanto was the baby of Sethka's family, two years younger than Dominique and not quite old enough to join the boys' lessons.

In all, Uncle Sethka had six sons and two daughters. The oldest boys, Himano, Finta, and Lerento were men themselves, already travelling in small groups with their donkeys and cicefyrian-wenches.

One day, Dominique thought, *I will be able to journey, too.* He would sell his Stories to the highest bidder. He would enthrall noblemen and kings with the historical stories he was learning now. Later, he would tell the tales he gathered from distant lands. He would bring back stories of wars and battles, angry neighbouring kings, and peasant farmers defeated by disease. He would breathe life into the people and events from far away for those who needed information from the farthest corners of the Known World: from beyond Kremland all the way up to the Polar North-lands, west across the Sea of Perfidium to Great Andalutania, east across the Sea of Chanmari to Ranginoor and the Festerworlds, and beyond that to Krokoska. . . .

"Dominique?" Uncle Sethka tapped his story stick impatiently across his thigh.

"Yes, sir?"

Uncle Sethka sighed and looked at Feltham. "Feltham, ask Dominique the question again since he wasn't listening."

"Can you stand like King Krokoska?"

Dominique looked at his uncle, surprised. Since joining the boys' group six weeks earlier, he had never been asked to demonstrate a stance. Still, how much harder could it be than imitating his mother? When she struck a pose and became Emanatio, the Goddess of Pure Water, and rose forth from beneath the ground, she seemed strong enough to force aside great boulders. He had seen his mother's transformations enough times before to know how it looked.

Dominique straightened his back and pushed out his chest, painfully aware of his slight frame so unlike the mighty king he was supposed to portray.

"Chin up. Yes. That's better. Think like a mighty warrior king."

Dominique's hand went to an imaginary weapon at his side. He moved his feet apart so he stood more solidly, as if he might actually do battle with anyone who came too near.

Uncle Sethka's deep, resonant voice began to tell a story. "And when, on the seventh night of the siege, King Krokoska ordered the drawbridge—"

Dominique knew what he was supposed to do. The story of King Krokoska and the drawbridge was one he had heard before. All he had to do was open his mouth and tell the next part of the story, tell how the king had ordered the drawbridge to be lowered. Dominique felt his shoulders slumping.

"King Krokoska ordered the drawbridge. . ." Sethka repeated.

"To be lowered," Feltham shouted. "Say it!"

"To . . . to . . . be . . ."

"To be lowered!" boomed Feltham. "Say it like a king!"

"Thank you, Feltham. That will be quite enough."

There was a long pause as Sethka waited for Dominique to say something. "Very well. Try again tomorrow. Rotiko?"

Feltham hissed his displeasure at not being chosen. Rotiko, dark eyes shining, stepped forward, regal and enthusiastic.

"King Krokoska ordered the drawbridge to be lowered," he declared, raising his arm as if giving an imperial command.

Sethka nodded and Rotiko continued, his voice strong and clear as he related the details of the battle that followed.

"The king strode forth, his great weapon swinging—left and right, *thwack, thump*—into the enemy soldiers."

"The enemies fell, one after the other, crying for mercy," Uncle Sethka added.

As Sethka and Rotiko took turns describing the battle, the other boys, too, joined in. Some made gasping sounds like dying men. Others shouted, "Be still, or die!" and "Sons of Lumpfish!" and "Evil be vanquished!" Feltham duelled with an imaginary opponent and Pickalotto whooped a blood-curdling cry as he charged towards his father, who continued to add detail after detail of the gory battle on the drawbridge until forty-seven soldiers lay dead or dying just outside the mountain fortress.

They are wonderful, Dominique thought as he listened, enthralled.

When the story was finally finished, Uncle Sethka gave Rotiko a nod and squeezed the boy's shoulder with his big, soft hand. "Fine work," he said. Turning to Dominique he added, "Another time, perhaps."

Dominique's ears burned crimson with shame. Next time he would speak up, he promised himself.

Later, at the evening meal, Dominique slipped away

from the boys to sit for a moment with his mother, lingering longer than necessary at her cooking fire.

"And?" she asked expectantly. "Was your day a little better?"

Dominique shrugged. Hardly. "A little. We told the story of King Krokoska." She didn't need to know he had been the only boy in the group who hadn't contributed to the story.

Dania nodded and scooped a sticky ball of bendahl pudding from the pot. Dominique's mouth began to water as she drizzled spiced oil over the top and handed him the wooden bowl.

"King Krokoska. Yes, a great king with many stories. Which one did you tell? About the treasures he hid in the Sea Caves of Krokoska?"

Dominique shook his head. "The one about the battle on the drawbridge."

"Hmm. Yes. You boys would have liked that one, I suppose."

"I should go back and eat with them," Dominique said as his three older sisters took their places around the family cooking fire, though the last place he wanted to eat was with the other boys.

"Did you hear a Story today?" Aegni asked.

"Shhh," Dania said. "Dominique and the other boys told the story of King Krokoska's battle of the drawbridge."

Dominique didn't correct her.

"But you've heard that one before," Simiaren said. "Aegni meant, did you hear a real—"

"Enough, Simiaren. Girls, take your food and be still."

No, Dominique thought, *I did not hear anything new.* Not only that, he couldn't even manage to tell a story all the men and boys knew well. He sighed. If only he had been able to become the great king, even for a few minutes. What kind of a teller would he ever be if he couldn't bring the people in his stories to life? That was bad enough, but even worse, he still could not do the most important thing of all—he could not hear the Stories from Beyond, the special Stories that gave Estorian men their privilege and power, the Stories for which wealthy kings would pay shiploads of gold. No, those Stories from Beyond eluded him.

"You are young, yet," Dania said, pushing his hair from his eyes. Dominique pulled away and walked back to join the other boys in his group.

He was only in his seventh year, he reminded himself. There was still plenty of time to learn. He lifted his bowl and drew in the rich aroma of stewed bendahl and spices. "Mmmm," he said, and settled with his back against a big simeon tree, its broad trunk still warm from a long afternoon in the sun. As he lifted his steaming bowl to his lips, the other boys moved away from him until he was the only one left sitting under the tree. He blew on his dinner and pretended he didn't care, but the meal had lost its taste and he had to struggle to finish it.

That night, Dominique lay on his sleeping mat in one corner of the family hut listening to his mother and sisters outside. The four women's voices rose and fell together, chanting beneath the stars.

Oh, glorious, glorious Viaticalla,
Goddess of Travels Afar—
our time of departure draws near,
your message—it swirls in the stars. . . .

Dominique listened to the familiar chant, wondering what message the stars held for his mother tonight.

Several other voices, all women, joined in the chorus.

Travel on?
Or bide our time?
Cherish this sanctuary?
Or travel on?

He knew that by the time the women finished, his mother would know whether the time had come to disband the camp and move on. After six months of nearly steady travel, the whole clan was ready to settle into a winter encampment on the south coast of Tanga.

Travel on?
Or bide our time . . ."

The steady click of pecka sticks played by the younger girls kept the rhythm going. Dominique buried his face in the soft moss-filled pillow his mother had made and drank in the smell of cool, dark woods.

"Stay here," he whispered to himself, fighting a longing to slip outside and join the women's circle. He was not a baby any more. His place was with the boys and then, someday, with the men.

Already he had spent more time with his mother than had any of the other boys. With his father gone so much and Uncle Sethka so busy, not only with his own sons but also with several other boys when their fathers were away, it was little wonder Dominique often felt pushed aside and in the way. Once the lessons were over for the day, it was just easier to stay away from everyone. The other boys didn't seem to care. Nobody ever sought out his company and he told himself that it didn't matter, that he didn't like the other boys, anyway.

Travel on?

Or bide our time . . .

Dominique pulled the pillow over his head and tried to shut out the sounds of the women chanting.

"Breathe," he told himself. "Breathe yourself into sleep."

Dania was already preparing the travel bundles when Dominique awoke the next morning.

"You must feed the tonnecks," she said as Dominique stood and stretched. "We're leaving for Tivarnen as soon as everything is ready." He watched for a moment as his mother tugged at the heavy flap of animal skins hanging over the entrance to the hut. Dominique's sisters, too, were up and busy making preparations for departure.

On a moving day, everyone in the clan had a job. The grannies took care of the infants, the men did the heavy work of dismantling the frames of the huts, and the women packed the bedding, cooking supplies, and fish traps. Dominique's job was to feed the tonnecks.

As he pushed clumps of grass through the vertical

sticks of their cages he fidgeted, willing the tonnecks to hurry up. "Come on. Eat faster." But nothing he said affected the slow-moving animals. They waddled deliberately to where he poked in their breakfast and chewed with unhurried concentration.

A little larger than wild rabbits, the tonnecks had huge, well-developed haunches. Those plump hindquarters were what made them such good eating. Their cat-like heads and big ears made them almost appealing, though Dominique knew how nasty they could be if mishandled. Their teeth were long and sharp and they weren't afraid to use them. The other lesson every tonneck-keeper learned quickly was that once the lid was opened, the tonnecks could move as fast as wild pistalots, bounding away before the tonneck-keeper knew what had happened.

Dominique moved from cage to cage, adding freshly picked grass to each. The clan had about fifty cages, each with a pair of tonnecks inside. The best breeders produced two litters of five or six kits each. The first litter was born in the very early spring. The young ones grew quickly and were slaughtered by the women once they reached about twelve weeks.

The second litter was usually born around the time of the autumn equinox. Dominique made sure to give the obviously pregnant females extra grass and fresh corpula berries to make sure they stayed healthy.

As soon as he'd finished feeding, Dominique

began loading the tonneck carts, carefully stacking the cages one atop the other.

"Need a hand?"

Dominique looked up at his cousin, Rotiko.

"Thanks," he said, a little warily.

Rotiko scrambled up onto the cart beside Dominique and together the two boys heaved a cage onto the top of the stack.

"At least this is the last time we have to do this job for a while," Rotiko said, squaring the cage so it sat properly on the one beneath.

Dominique nodded.

"Do you know what mask you'll be making this winter?" Rotiko asked. Dominique shook his head. There would be plenty of time at the Tivarnen camp for the boys to work on the masks, costumes, and drums they would use in their storytelling.

"No. I haven't thought about it yet."

Rotiko cocked his head to the side and looked at Dominique. "You are a bit slow, aren't you? Just like Feltham said."

Dominique ignored the jibe and picked up one end of a tonneck cage.

"I'm going to make a mask of King Sim so I can tell the story of the Battle for High Chem."

"I haven't heard that one," Dominique admitted.

"My father told me," Rotiko said. "You don't know it?"

"Grab the other end, would you?" Dominique answered, lifting one end of the next tonneck cage. He didn't want to argue with Rotiko who, though younger than Dominique, was considerably heavier.

"Slow as one of Gellebem's snails," Rotiko said as he lifted the other end of the cage.

Dominique gave the cage a push and the other boy stumbled. "Oh, so sorry," Dominique said.

Rotiko drew his lips back in a snarl and growled deep in his throat like an angry sear-cat. "Don't think you can get away with pushing me around," he said. "Your father is such a coward he dares not return to camp."

"Shut up!" Dominique shoved the cage just as Rotiko was climbing up into the cart and the other boy fell backwards. He sat down heavily, twisted out from underneath the cage on his lap, and leaped off the cart on top of Dominique.

The impact sent Dominique flying into the grass and the two boys scrambled to try to get the upper hand. Rotiko was heavier and stronger but Dominique was quick and nimble. They wrestled, shrieking and cursing. Dominique swung wildly and his fist crunched into Rotiko's nose.

"Boys!"

Both boys jumped apart and straightened up, Rotiko's hand covering his bleeding nose. Dominique gulped for breath, feeling slightly sick at the sight of the blood dribbling between Rotiko's fingers.

Roman Bertolescu glowered at the culprits.

"Rotiko. To your father—he is loading the water barrels."

Rotiko bobbed his head and hurried away.

"Dominique—your father would be ashamed."

Dominique dropped his eyes and stared at the long ears of the tonneck in the closest cage. "Yes, sir." He waited to hear what his punishment would be, but Bertolescu only sighed.

"Finish loading. By yourself."

"Yes, sir."

Dominique waited until the Protector's footsteps had retreated back towards the group of men who were taking apart the huts. Then, rubbing his shoulder, he bent over the next tonneck cage to be loaded and muttered, "Papa. Come home before . . ." He couldn't finish the thought. If his father didn't come home soon, what new torments would the boys dream up?

Working alone, it took ages to stack the rest of the cages onto the carts that the older boys would then pull to the next camp. Drenched with sweat, Dominique clambered back on top of the first cart and stretched a light woven mat made of young, supple chellabong reeds over the top of the stacked cages.

The weave was so close it not only provided shade but also kept the tonnecks dry in case of a sudden downpour.

By the time Dominique had loaded the carts and secured the matting, two of the men had dismantled the three-sided shelter where the tonneck cages were kept while the clan was in camp.

Long before the sun reached its midday zenith, the entire camp had completely disappeared. Even the stones of the central fire circle had been scattered. The ashes, animal bones, and any bits and pieces of broken pots or other refuse had been buried. Once the flattened grass where the huts had stood had grown again, it would be nearly impossible to tell a group of more than fifty had stayed there.

Those men who were in camp and not off on storytelling travels loaded the heaviest gear into sturdy carts pulled by equally sturdy Festerworld donkeys. The tough little animals were strong and hardy, if sometimes a little lazy.

Everyone, man, woman, and child, carried a bundle of some sort or pulled a cart laden with gear. Even the oldest of the grannies were able to manage a light straw mat, bundle of kindling, or a small baby.

With all preparations for departure completed, Protector Bertolescu raised his staff and stood in the centre of what had been the main fire circle.

> *Oh, Keepers of great Wisdom from Beyond,*
> *watch over this place until our people*
>   *return.*
> *Keep us well on our journey*
> *and let us find our destination waiting,*
>   *ready.*

All the clan members clapped twice and shouted, "With thanks, we journey on!"

With the silence appropriate to all departures, nobody else spoke as bundles were lifted to backs, shoulders leaned into harnesses, and many pairs of feet fell into line as the Estorian clan of Bertolescu turned south and headed for the winter camp nearest to the village of Tivarnen.

CHAPTER

3

WINTER AT TIVARNEN

*Tara knelt before the group of boys and bowed
her head. "Go then," she said, "and find your
Stories. I shall keep the fire burning."*

The Tivarnen camp at the southernmost end of the
island of Tanga was one of the clan's favourites.
Good, clear water tumbled in twin streams that
flanked either side of the camp before spilling into
the sea. A sheltered cove close by provided drift-
wood for firewood and building, seaweed for cooking,
and plenty of succulent rookles, tender shellfish
that buried themselves into the soft sand of the
beach.

Once camp had been established, the Estorians
settled into their winter routine. The women, who
had carefully tucked glowing coals in sacred clay
fire pots for the journey, lit and tended the cooking
fires, foraged for tembeh roots, collected berries,

and prepared strips of tonneck for smoking. The boys, working in groups according to age, began each morning with lessons in contemplation and stillness. Those men who remained in camp worked with the boys as they perfected their storytelling techniques.

"A quiet mind is a place where Stories will find nourishment," Uncle Sethka said. He moved among the boys in Dominique's lesson group as they sat cross-legged and motionless.

"It is no longer enough to gather Story fragments without understanding their deeper meaning. But for the Stories to take shape, your minds must be still and peaceful."

Dominique peeked across the circle at Feltham, whose mouth sagged open and arms hung limply at his sides.

"Dominique! Eyes shut!"

Dominique jumped. He squeezed his eyes shut and tried hard to think of nothing.

How did the other boys do it? How did they shut out all the things that had happened during the past days and weeks? Botta Kendako's father had just returned from a voyage to Sedna, the island to the north where Lord Penalto ruled. Botta's father had told stories of the way Lord Penalto kept adding to his fortress, building the walls higher with sand-stone shipped from the cliffs of High Chem on the mainland. His latest addition to his fortress was a series of giant vats set along the battlements. Each great iron cauldron was large enough to hold a warhorse and was suspended from a huge wooden arm the guards could swing out over the castle walls.

When the vat, loaded with a mixture of boulders and boiling oil, was tipped using a system of ropes and pulleys, the deadly mixture tumbled down onto the heads of any attackers who dared attempt to scale the castle walls.

Dominique imagined an army of men, sailing on tall-masted schooners from Ranginoor. King Sim of Castle Donemicci, high in the mountains of Ranginoor, would lead his men to a hidden bay at the east end of Sedna.

"Men!" King Sim raised his hand and his men froze, the whites of their eyes shining in the moonlight. From then on, the attack was carried out in silence using only hand signals. Stealthily, King Sim's army crept towards the base of the castle walls, not knowing about Lord Penalto's new weapons—

"And, at the count of five, bring your minds back to a state of clarity."

Back into focus? Dominique's mind had never been unclear. The images of King Sim's men had been as vivid as if the army lived and marched inside his head.

"Now, boys. We shall travel the circle and hear from each of you how it felt to be of still mind and open heart."

Dominique hoped fervently that he would not be called upon to speak first.

"Feltham?"

The boy opposite Dominique stood, unfolding

his long legs and stretching his arms out at his sides.

"Emp-ti-nesssss," Feltham said, pulling his arms wider apart as if stretching the word between his hands.

"Did you see any images?" Uncle Sethka asked.

Feltham shook his head. "Nothing. Nothing at all." His arms fell to his sides and he dropped his head, all humility and innocence. "And for that, I am most thankful."

"As well you should be," Sethka said.

"Aye!" agreed a man striding towards the group. The boys looked around.

"Papa!" Feltham cried and ran to his father, who laughed and scooped the boy into his arms.

"Hey! You are nearly too big for this!"

Feltham squirmed free from his father's hold and dropped to the ground beside him.

"May I take him from the circle?"

Dominique winced as the taller version of Feltham ruffled his fingers affectionately through his son's hair.

"Certainly. Welcome back. I am most pleased with your boy's progress."

Feltham beamed.

"Shall I see you both at tomorrow's lessons?"

"Aye, yes. For as long as I remain in camp, the boy shall not leave my side."

For the next several weeks, groups of men returned to the village. Those with sons joined the lessons and the pace of learning picked up as each shared his specialties with the eager students.

Kem, Marcus, Botta, and Feltham all sat alongside their fathers for at least part of each day. Their masks, their costumes, their retellings of the old tales were far better than Dominique's efforts, despite the fact that all the men took turns helping him.

Each day, Dominique scanned the two tracks leading into camp, hoping a distant smudge of dust might grow and become solid and take the shape of his own father.

The weeks passed in a blur of lessons as the boys learned new voice techniques, and beat drums to pull the sounds of rain, marching, or warfare from the air around them. But still, there was no sign of Boris Elnedo. Dominique's mother would say nothing when he hounded her for information. When would he return? Dominique thought of Lord Penalto's vats of boiling boulders. Could something have happened to his father? Dominique pestered his mother with questions.

"Hush. In good time he shall return. Concentrate on your lessons so when he does come back he will have much to be proud of."

All through the winter Dominique did work hard. He found he had a natural flair for working with his hands. Sethka praised his mask of the sea dragon, Cho, and made a point of showing it to Protector Bertolescu. But, though Dominique tried again and again, whenever he was asked to come forward and tell part of a Story he found himself hopelessly tongue-tied.

Gradually, the boys were encouraged to invite visions to come to them when they were in a state of quiet concentration. These visions, flashes of images and Stories, would eventually lead to the clear reception and understanding of the great Stories from Beyond.

Diligently, Dominique nurtured his inner still-ness every day, even sometimes as he lay in bed at night, but no matter how he concentrated he could not seem to control his mind. Some of the men had left again and others had drifted back to the encampment, and Dominique thought of their stories of places they had been: the Festerworlds, where there was great unrest and reports of Camprianos moving east from West Ermes with building materials, and Krokoska, where the High Queen Mafusellia had declared her intention to send forth explorers to chart the mountains of Great Andalutania far across the Sea of Perfidium.

On Ticabella, one of the small islands at the north end of the Drasil Archipelago, Kem's father had been stung by a kretchnat beetle when he rolled onto it in his sleep.

"The pain!" he had cried, re-enacting the scene by the evening fire. "My thigh was swollen to five times its normal size." He showed how engorged his leg had become by spreading his fingers wide and holding his hands apart. "Madness-making, head-bursting, fire-burning-in-my-very-veins kinds of pain." He moaned and groaned, thrashing on the ground, his hands clutching at his thigh.

"If the Mirrah-folk hadn't found me, I suppose I should never have returned."

Not only had the group of healers drawn the

poison from his wound by sucking on his leg and spitting the poison onto the ground (a part of the story Kem's father told with great drama), they had given him a small vial of kretchnat beetle anti-venom. The bottle had joined the others in Dania's healing collection.

These stories, brought home by the men and told with such gusto, filled Dominique's head and he found it impossible to push them away, to hold his mind completely still and empty so Stories from Beyond might enter.

Whenever Uncle Sethka asked Dominique to describe his stillness, Dominique had to admit he had found only the marvellous stories the other men had brought back from their travels.

"Dominique," Uncle Sethka said one morning after Dominique admitted once again he had failed to find calm. "You must take this more seriously or you will never learn to hear Stories from Beyond."

Behind Sethka, Feltham stuck his fingers in his ears and pulled a face.

"Dominique. Look at me."

Dominique looked up at Uncle Sethka's face. Deep lines crinkled around the older man's eyes and Dominique wanted to ask why they were forcing him to do this when he obviously couldn't hear any new Stories and had no ability to tell the old ones, either. Why couldn't Sethka make an exception and let him tell the Tara stories he had learned from his mother?

But he knew such questions would be pointless. The Tara stories might be barely acceptable for very young boys to tell, and they could help a boy get started learning delivery techniques—but by now he should be putting those stories out of his mind and telling the stories of men, the stories he would someday need to earn a living.

The whole *point* of learning to be a great teller among Estorians was so a man could do a respectable job of telling the real Stories of Truth, those that came from the Place Beyond, those that guided kings and ended wars.

"Dominique—you *must* learn to do this. You *will* learn to hear the Stories meant for you."

Uncle Sethka tapped Dominique lightly on the shoulder. "Go now and find a place by the stream. Stay still and listen until you hear nothing. Do you understand?"

Dominique nodded, his thin shoulders round, his fingers opening and closing on the soft fabric of his cotton leggings. He turned and walked away, trying to shut out the taunts and jeers of the other boys.

"Boys!" Sethka's voice silenced the others. "Let us return to work on finding and shaping our Stories from Beyond."

In time, the men set out on more journeys, taking their Stories with them. Spring arrived with the warm wash of moist ocean breezes. The women chanted and the Estorians moved on, travelling up the west coast of Tanga, stopping at the western ceremonial grounds to meet with other Estorian clans for the great Coming of Stories Ceremony for boys in their thirteenth year. Then the clans split up once again and Dominique's people travelled across the strait to Sedna. There they spent the long, hot summer travelling through Lord Penalto's lands so that the younger men and the older boys could hone their skills by telling stories in the villages and marketplaces of the countryside.

As the autumn equinox drew near, the women chanted and determined they must head south once again and return to the southern reaches of Tanga where the winters were mildest and the returning men would know where to find their families.

And so the Estorian migrations continued north to south and north again as the clan of Bertolescu followed the seasons, collected stories, and the men sold words of inspired wisdom to those willing to pay for Stories from Beyond.

4

THE COMING OF THE KASYAPA BIRD

If the colours of the kasyapa bird remain bright, good fortune will shine throughout the land.

"Hey! Mutondo boy!" Feltham yelled from down in the valley.

Dominique crouched behind Tall Sentry, the largest of the five large rocks overlooking the new encampment in the Sumbalon Valley.

"Shut up," Dominique whispered.

"Baby boy! Baby mute boy!"

"Shut up, shut up, shut up," Dominique said, but quietly, in case they should come pounding up the hill, find him, and pummel his ears until the pain in his head made him want to scream.

"Hey, mutondo! Where are you?"

"Go away. Go away."

Belly pressed to the ground, he wiggled closer to the huge boulder. Peering around the rock he could just make out Feltham, Kem, Marcus, and the other boys his age. *Swish, swish,* they swung sticks through the tall grasses, looking for him.

He watched them come together in a little group, their heads bobbing up and down. For a few moments their sticks hung still beside them.

"Yes, go. Go without me."

The boys looked around once more and then turned and trotted off towards the cart track leading to the village of Barenta. Dominique closed his eyes and let out a long, slow breath.

Good. The rest of the afternoon was his. He rolled onto his side and looked down the steep hill behind him to the level area by the stream where his clan had been camped for the past two weeks. He stretched out his arm and raised his thumb so it blotted out Protector Bertolescu's large hut at the northernmost tip of the circle. When he closed one eye, the hut jumped to the side and he moved his thumb over until it was hidden again. By opening first one eye and then the other, Dominique made the hut jump from side to side, over and over.

A movement from the other side of the circle caught his eye and he sat up to see better. His mother tied back the door flap of the family hut. When Dominique stood in that doorway he looked directly across the circle to the Protector's door. It was no comfort to Dominique when his mother said, "He watches over us. Especially over you."

The Protector knew when Dominique left the encampment and when he returned. He would have to stay hidden in the hills until the other boys returned from Barenta.

Dominique plucked a tall stalk of grass and slipped the hard, sweet end into his mouth. Gnawing on it thoughtfully he wondered how long he was going to be able to get away with hiding from the boys. If Uncle Sethka found out he wasn't going to the village to take part in the Storytelling circle with the other boys, he would be furious. Sethka would tell his mother and Bertolescu. Then, the Protector would call a punishment circle and Dominique would be sent off to spend an afternoon cleaning tonneck cages or sweeping out the Protector's hut. Dominique sighed. He was getting to know the dusty corners of Bertolescu's hut all too well.

But going into the village was even worse. The treks to the village square always ended up the same way. When it came time for Dominique to step forward into the centre of the boys' circle, to take the story stick in his hand and tell a Story, the same thing always happened: nothing. Then the jeering would start—"mutondo boy" or "baby boy" or worse. He'd be lucky if he escaped with a couple of shoves. Sometimes it was much worse—scrapes and bruises, and so often, the ringing in his ears after they smacked him on the head, supposedly to clear his hearing passages so he, too, could hear Stories from Beyond.

At ten, the other boys were all so good now. On

demand they could call a Story from Beyond, shape it, and then tell it with skill that nearly rivalled that of the travelling men. It wouldn't be long now before all the boys in his lesson group would come before the gathered clans during the boys' Coming of Stories Ceremony to show all they had learned and prove they were competent enough to begin travelling and earning their keep.

Dominique sighed again, trying to ignore the slow, sad twisting he felt deep in his gut.

A rustle behind him startled him and he leaped to his feet and turned around.

"Who's there?"

He couldn't see anything.

"Hello?"

Heart hammering, he held his breath, listening. He had heard something moving through the tall grasses. One of the boys creeping up behind him? Could one of the women from the encampment have strayed so far in search of firewood? Then an even worse thought came to him. A snake? Could it be a snake? A poisonous black-headed rialox?

Dominique backed away from where he had heard the noise until he felt the cool, sharp edges of Tall Sentry hard against his shoulder blades.

"Hello?"

Slowly, his heart began to beat more smoothly. It was nothing. Just the wind. Didn't his mother say that guilt sharpened the nerves?

"Agggh!"

Dominique flung himself sideways, twisting away from the whirling demon that shot out of the grass towards him. He scuttled along in front of the rocks, trying to find a way to squeeze through, looking for a place he could hide. The rocks that had protected him from the eyes of the boys now prevented his escape.

"Mama!" he shrieked and the sound behind him stopped. Down in the encampment, his mother had disappeared. Maybe she had heard him—maybe she would come and save him. He squeezed his eyes shut. Prickles ran up and down his back as he imagined the poisonous claws of the demon raking his bare skin. The sun beat down on his back—why hadn't he listened to his mother when she told him to wear his cotton tunic?

Rigid with fear, Dominique clutched at the stone in front of him. He promised himself that if he survived this attack he would crawl back down to the encampment, find Protector Bertolescu, and confess that he'd been hiding. Any punishment would be better than—

He didn't have a chance to formulate a clear picture of his demise because he became aware of another sound coming from behind him some- where down on the ground. Something wheezed softly and every few seconds there was a rustle and a moan.

Dominique racked his brains, trying to remember if any of the clan stories told about a creature that made such sounds before attacking. The river serpent, Lagrace, sang to her victims and the White Bear of Orus always gave a warning grunt. The yagabonos of the high plains weren't

45

noisy, but you could smell them long before you spotted them. He remained motionless, pressed up against the rock. His left leg began to quiver with the strain of standing so awkwardly and he waited several minutes before he decided the sound wasn't getting any closer and it would be safe enough to ease his left foot back a little so it was flat on the ground.

If anything, the wheezing and whiffling was softer now. It didn't really sound threatening—not remotely like a growl or a roar or even a grunt. *Whooozzeeee.* It was more like the sound something made when it was in pain, or ill. The wheezing reminded Dominique of the way Granny Poona had sounded in the final days before she died.

Surely the animal or demon or whatever it was would have attacked by now. What harm could it do to at least catch a glimpse of it before it leaped on him?

Jaw clenched, Dominique held on firmly to the rock and slowly turned his head until he could see the edge of something on the ground directly behind him. Like a piece of light cloth, the thing rippled up and down with each wheezy noise it made, but because it was right behind him, Dominique still couldn't make out exactly what it was.

The thing flipped up and Dominique gasped, turning his head back so quickly he grazed his cheek against the rock. "Ow!" Startled by the sharp pain, he raised his hand to his face and his fingertips came away smeared with red. He staggered sideways, turning as he went, intending to fend off the creature when it jumped on him.

What he saw on the ground brought him to a complete stop, the sting in his cheek no longer important. There before him, struggling to breathe, was a full-grown kasyapa bird. About the size of a dove but with long tail feathers, it quivered and wheezed on the ground before him. He dropped to his knees and reached out his hand, but weak though the bird was, it fluttered away, wings and feathers whirling in the sun.

It disappeared into the grass, clumsily thrashing its way through the waving stalks just ahead of Dominique. This was not the magnificent bird of iridescent plumage he had heard about in so many stories, but a pale creature, virtually transparent and unable, apparently, to fly. The only reason he knew for certain it was a kasyapa bird was the bright red crest atop its head. These few feathers alone remained bright and when he was too slow to follow, the bird raised its crest and fixed Dominique in its stare so he had no choice but to hurry along to where it wanted to take him.

Before long they arrived at another outcropping of boulders. The tops of the rocks were higher than Dominique's head and smeared with bird droppings. On the flat top of one was a nest of sticks and grass, its sides high enough to form a deep bowl. The bird lay at the base of the stone, looking up at Dominique, and he knew he must climb up and look into the nest. Bashing his knees and elbows against the rock as he climbed, he inched his way up the boulder. Feeling for cracks and handholds with his fingers and toes, he heaved himself over the top edge of the stone pillar and raised himself high enough to see inside the mud-smeared nest.

The blood-red throat of a baby bird gaped at him.

"I don't have anything," he said. At the sound of his voice the chick began to scream, loud piercing alarm cries that Dominique thought could surely be heard all the way in the village.

"Shhh . . . I'm going to help you," he said, though until that very moment he had no idea he was going to do any such thing.

He crawled forward until he was kneeling on the flat top of the boulder, raised himself up, and leaned over the nest. Slowly he reached inside to pick up the baby bird.

"Ow!" His finger flew to his mouth and he sucked on it, amazed at how much the chick's nip had hurt.

"Come on. Let me help you." He tried again, but once more the bird's beak darted out and bit him hard, this time on the fleshy heel of his hand. He waved his hand around and shouted.

"Stop that! I'm trying to help you!"

He crouched beside the nest, panting lightly, his forehead furrowed. Back down at the base of the rock, the mother bird lay in the dust, her sides heaving with each laboured breath, her head lifting weakly every few gasps when she tried to look up at the nest.

"I should have worn my shirt. Then I could have wrapped you in it and carried you home. Mama will know how to help you." He spoke quietly, calming the young bird. Unlike its mother, the nestling did not yet have a crest of scarlet feathers. Its plumage was still downy and the colour of goldenrod. Dominique wondered when the baby bird's brilliant feathers would emerge. Stories of the kasyapa birds always spoke of their extraordinary colours—rich blues, greens, and yellows. The birds were so stunning as they flashed across the sky, they had caused grown men to fall from their horses in astonishment.

But they were so rare. Very few had ever seen one, and those who had, never missed an opportunity to speak of it. Dominique glanced down at the mother bird still lying on the ground below. This baby, still too young to fly, would never survive alone.

"How am I going to get you home?"

He looked down at his baggy trousers and then searched the deserted grassy hills. Interrupted only by occasional rocky outcroppings, the landscape was quite empty.

Nobody would see him. Balancing on the rocky ledge beside the nest, he peeled off his soft cotton pants and put his hands into the trouser legs. Very carefully, he dropped the trousers over the bird's head and then gathered up the squirmy bundle in both hands. The screeching sounds from inside the cloth made it sound like he was wringing the bird's neck, and Dominique's face scrunched up as he cringed from the noise.

"Shhhh . . ." He pressed the bundle to his chest and held it there with one hand while he scrambled back down the rock. He jumped the last little bit and landed in the dirt just beside the mother bird.

He crouched beside her. The body was still and the wheezing had stopped.

"May you find your place over the Jade Bridge," he whispered. Gently he reached out to touch her lovely feathers, now as white as any swan's. Even her crest had faded so there was not a hint of pink in the feathers. Leaving his bundle on the ground for a few minutes, he moved the mother bird's body to the side, amazed at how light it was, like a shadow or a memory of a living thing. He found enough rocks to make a circle around the kasyapa bird and then piled another row of rocks on top. Adding stones until there was a small mound covering the bird, he stepped back to admire his work. At least this way the bird would not be devoured by the buzzards already circling slowly overhead.

Worried about the baby, Dominique carefully placed a last, flat stone over the top of the cairn and hurried to scoop up his trousers, his precious find wrapped inside.

CHAPTER

5

THE ELEVENTH YEAR OF SILENCE

The great teller, Tebano, left the king's palace
with a wagonload of gold.
If only he had shared his wealth, perhaps he
would not have died the way he did,
a single dagger thrust deep into his heart.

"Dominique! What are you doing here? Where are your pants?"

Dominique turned when his mother's frame in the opening dimmed the light in the hut. At first, she didn't see the bundle behind him.

"Mama! Look!"

"Your face! What happened?"

"Nothing. I fell against a rock."

"Where are the other boys? Why aren't you—"

"Look."

He moved aside and waved his arm at his bundle of trousers and bird he had tucked into the family's largest wooden grinding bowl.

"I'll build it some kind of nest. What does it eat?"

"Dominique!" Dania's hand flew to her mouth. "You can't keep this! Kasyapa birds are . . . they are wild things. Powerful creatures. You know that." Her hand snapped forward and cuffed him on the side of the head. "Have you learned nothing? How could you rob a nest?"

Dominique's eyes stung. "The mother bird tried to lead me—"

"Tried to lead you away from her baby—yes, I'm sure she did. And you just thought you were so clever not to follow her. I can't believe you would—"

"No! That's not what happened." Through sobs, and stopping only to wipe his running nose with the back of his hand, Dominique told her how the dying kasyapa bird had led him to the nest.

"I have never heard of such a thing," she said when he was done. But her anger was gone and she gently lifted the trousers away from the bird so she could inspect it more closely. "Poor little thing. It looks hungry."

"So I can keep it?"

"One never keeps a wild thing. When it has fully grown, I'm sure it will leave. But a kasyapa bird? I can't believe the mother bird found you—showed herself to you." Dania twiddled the end of a long strand of hair around her finger, running her thumb over and around the beads at the end. "A kasyapa bird." She shook her head. "Well, if you have been chosen to care for this little one, then you must do the best you can."

Dominique grinned.

"But only until it chooses to leave."

Together, they lined a deep basket with moss, but when Dania tried to help Dominique transfer the bird into its new nest, it screamed and protested until Dania moved aside and Dominique did it himself. The bird panted but didn't try to bite Dominique when he gingerly moved her into the basket. Dania showed Dominique how to grind a paste of brimble berries and add crushed mealy worms and tembeh root. The bird's mouth snapped open when Dominique offered a bit of the sticky mixture on the end of a stick. He dropped a bit at a time down the pink gullet, careful to hold the very end of the stick, well out of the way of the snapping beak.

"Not too much all at once," his mother cautioned from a distance. "You'll have to feed a small amount and often."

When the bird was full and resting in the moss, Dania inspected the graze on her son's cheek.

"Why didn't you go with the other boys? You were supposed to be at the village, taking part in the Storytelling."

Dominique looked away, not wanting to disappoint his mother again.

"I should tell Sethka . . . and the Protector."

Dominique said nothing. She was right, of course. He should be punished even though it was her—. He stopped the thought and swallowed guiltily. It wasn't really his mother's fault that Dominique had to spend long days with boys who hated him. He couldn't blame her that week after week he was the only one whose father never came to visit, the only one who could not seem to entice Stories into his head. Even so, he pulled away, angry with her for not making things different.

"Hold still. Let me clean this properly."

Wincing, he closed his eyes as she dabbed at the graze on his cheek. "You must learn to get along with the others. They are so talented. Ask for their help and they will teach you."

Her words were hollow, familiar, and useless. Four years was more than long enough to receive any help the boys might wish to give him. But in the four years since he had been forbidden to help his mother with her chores, the others had simply perfected new ways of tormenting and excluding him.

"I have heard your father will return before the autumn equinox," Dania said quietly.

"Really?" Dominique despised his own weakness. How could he allow himself to be so easily distracted?

"Sit still or the salve will go in your eye."

"Papa is coming back?"

Dania nodded, smoothing on the healing honey-balm with her thumb.

"Will he stay this time? How many weeks before the equinox?"

"There. I'm finished." She shrugged and Dominique moved away. "I don't know if he will stay. It just depends on . . . it just depends. But it won't be long now. Three weeks."

The questions and their half-hidden accusations tumbled out.

"Why is he away more than Feltham's father?

Last time he was here for only one night and then—"
Dominique's voice broke. "Then, gone again." He
spat the words out, their taste bitter and dirty in his
mouth. "He's away more than . . . more than . . ."

Dominique didn't go on. He could have said any
boy's name. Nobody's father was away more often
or for longer than his.

"Boris Elnedo has important Stories to tell."

"Important how?"

"You are too young to understand. Besides, they
are men's Stories. You know very well I can't tell them
to you. Perhaps when he is here you can ask him."

Dominique nodded, though he didn't think for a
minute he would actually ask his father anything.
The man was a giant—huge, with blond hair down
to his shoulders. His big, powerful hands looked
strong enough to crush rocks to powder just like
the giant, Cragor, in the stories. Boris Elnedo might
be a wonderful Storyteller when he travelled to
distant courts and cities, but when he did, occasionally, return to his people, he seemed a haunted
man, restless and uneasy with one eye always on
the path leading from the camp.

Even when, during a short visit late in
Dominique's eighth year, he had asked Dominique,
"Son, tell me, have the Stories started to come?" he
hadn't looked his son in the eye. When Dominique
had admitted failure, his father's face had grown
taut and still as if he had wanted to tell Dominique
something, but couldn't. And there was still the
matter of the Namingstone. Boris Elnedo had not yet
left his mark on Dominique's stone. When, once,

Dominique had started to ask his father about it, he could not make himself form the question. By the following morning, his father had disappeared again.

"I don't want him to come back."

"You don't mean that."

"Yes, I do."

"Come here."

Dominique tried to stand his ground, but could not resist Dania's open arms. He stumbled forward, surprising himself by sobbing. She held him for a long time, rocking him slowly from side to side until, finally, his fists unclenched and his breathing slowed.

"Your father is one of the wisest tellers of all time. He is the reason we have this position in the circle."

Dominique knew he should feel honoured to live in the hut erected at the southernmost point of the encampment circle. It was the second most powerful position, after Protector Bertolescu's hut on the northern side.

"The boys hate me more because we live here."

"They are jealous, Dominique."

"And it's not fair. *I* can't even hear the shortest, easiest Story. I should be jealous of *them*." He *was* jealous of them. He hated them all.

"Shhhh . . ." She waited until the new sobs subsided.

"Why can't I hear the Stories? Why?"

"You will, my son. You will. Perhaps this bird is an omen." She paused. "I have never heard of a kasyapa bird living with people. It is special."

He looked up at her through his tears.

"As she grows, perhaps you can practise. Maybe you just need the right kind of audience."

Dominique swallowed his disappointment. A bird couldn't understand Stories, even if he had any to tell. Besides, hadn't his mother said the bird would fly off the minute it had all its feathers? The bird was useless.

"I'll ask Protector Bertolescu if you can stay here while the bird is small—I'm too busy to care for it. If you think it would help you tell your Stories, I'm sure he will let you."

Dominique nodded. He didn't think for a moment it would work, but anything was better than being sent out each day with the boys. The daily lessons had ended for a time. Uncle Sethka was preparing to leave on a short trip to the port of Corposcia, and the boys' task while he was gone was to visit the closest village and perform before local audiences who tended to be enthusiastic and appreciative of the boys' efforts.

Dania leaned over the baby bird and smiled. "Perhaps you should give her a name so we don't have to keep calling her 'the bird.'"

"Navina." The name of the Goddess of Clarity flew from Dominique's lips.

Dania smiled and Dominique sat beside her. She put her arm around his shoulders and gave him a squeeze.

"Why didn't Papa come back for the equinox, Mama?"

"Shhh. Go to sleep."

"You said he would be here." Maybe it was his

fault. Maybe his father wouldn't come back until he could be proud of his only son.

Dania sighed. "There is trouble in the city of Carnillo."

"What kind of trouble?" Dominique closed his eyes, trying to push away images of the filthy port city and the dangers that lurked in her streets. "Is that where he has gone? To Carnillo?"

"He is working with the Lord of Grenille . . . It is not my place to speak of it." She folded her hands together. "I've said too much already. Your father will tell you when he comes back."

"When? When will he be back?"

Dominique heard her shifting beneath her heavy woven blanket. "It may take some time. But I would think he will return before your Coming of Stories Ceremony. He should come to give you a story stick."

Dominique's mouth opened in horror. He forced it closed again, glad of the distance and the darkness between them so she would not see his misery. The ceremony was a year and a half away! She couldn't seriously think he would not see his father again before then?

He shut his eyes and tried to conjure a clear picture of the last time his father had come home. Nothing. What he saw instead was his father leaving, so long ago—shortly after his ninth birthday. It had been raining and his father, astride a horse and leading a mule, had turned and waved at him. One night. That was all the time he had spent at the encampment. One short night.

There had been others with him when he left

the last time—Feltham Tomonok's father for one, and Kem's uncle Rogan. But the others had returned and gone again several times since. Only his father had stayed away.

Why? And why had the few visits he had actually made over the years been so short? What had the frantic, whispered conversations with Protector Bertolescu and the other adults been about?

He waited in the dark and listened to his mother's breathing as it slowed and deepened to match the rhythm of his sleeping sisters. A soft clicking came from the basket beside him on the floor. It was Navina, clicking her beak.

Dominique reached his hand out in the dark. He no longer had to worry about being bitten. It hadn't taken the bird long to discover he was the source of tasty food, and she had become quite friendly. Navina shifted a little closer to his hand. Dominique stretched out a finger and very gently rubbed the feathers on the back of her head. Nearly all her adult plumage, including a fiery red crest atop her head, had grown in now. He pulled his hand back under the blanket, ignoring her mutters of protest. It wouldn't be long before she was flying properly and then she, too, would be gone.

His hand went to the stone talisman he wore around his neck, the only stone in the whole clan bearing only the marks of women. In disgust, he let it go and turned his face to the wall of the hut. His father hadn't been at his Naming Ceremony and had never bothered to add his mark since. He had no reason to believe he would return for the Coming of Stories.

6

PREPARATION

*The dragon roared and mothers rushed
forward to offer up their naughty children.
The first to go were those without Stories.*

"Ready, Dominique?" Dania pushed Dominique's
thick tumble of blond curls away from his eyes.

Dominique tugged at the loose folds of his ceremonial feather tunic. He would never be ready.

"Tuck some of this up under the belt. Stand still."

No matter how his mother fiddled, the
borrowed tunic didn't fit. It was far too big.

"Did you say thank you to Uncle Sethka?"

Dominique nodded. He shouldn't have said thank
you to anyone but his father. If his father had been
there, he would have made sure the tunic fit properly.

*The tunic passed from hand to hand, father
to son. And in every feather there lay a Story, and in
every Story, a vision for the future. . . .*

"You have grown so tall this winter." Dania hugged her son to her, and it was all Dominique could do to hold his back stiff and keep his arms at his sides. "Where's Navina?"

Dominique whistled and the kasyapa bird flew down from her perch up on the ridgepole. She landed on his shoulder with a ruffle of shimmering blue-green feathers.

"Inside," he said, and Navina wriggled into a pouch sewn like a deep pocket inside the waist of his baggy cotton underleggings. Navina settled in her place against his hip, her soft warmth a familiar comfort.

Dania shook her head in disbelief. Though she no longer spoke of Navina's leaving, Dominique knew his mother didn't understand why Navina stayed. Dominique didn't really understand either, but with each month that passed with Navina close by, he worried less that she would someday fly off and leave him.

"Boys! Boys, all boys—I call the boys!"

Dominique and his mother turned their heads towards the sound of Protector Bertolescu's voice.

"I don't want to—"

"Shhh. Touch your Namingstone when you need to find peace."

Dominique's fingers rose halfway to the stone hanging in its pouch around his neck. He gazed around the tent, the last time he would see the inside of his mother's home. After the Coming of Stories Ceremony he would move into the long home, the place where boys finished the journey to manhood together.

His throat tightened. "What if I can't . . ."

"Shhh. Of course your Story will come to you. We have used the hen's oil cure behind your ears."

He grimaced at the thought of the sticky mixture of grouse fat, ground garlic and lamb's urine his mother had insisted on smearing behind his ears morning and night.

"And haven't you told me you have learned to be still?"

That hadn't been a lie. Dominique had become very good at stillness, at holding his mind empty, ready for Stories to pour into him. He flicked his tongue over his dry lips. Unfortunately, nothing had yet filled the stillness.

"I think the Keepers of Stories must have a very special Story for you to tell. That's why they've waited this long. You'll see. They won't disappoint you."

"Boys, boys! I call forth all boys!"

Dania smiled and kissed her son on the forehead.

"Prepare well, my child. For tomorrow we may listen, listen."

Dominique turned and stumbled out of the tent into the gathering darkness. All the boys in their thirteenth year and Rotiko in his twelfth emerged from the other huts and moved towards the centre of the circle, where Protector Bertolescu waited with a smoky torch. When all the boys had gathered, Bertolescu cleared his throat and raised the torch high, holding it over each boy in turn.

"And so, your journey to manhood begins tonight."

The boys stopped moving. Dominique's hand went to the bird tucked inside the pouch at his side.

"Understand you may not burden your bodies with food or drink until after dark tomorrow night."

"We abide by the will of the Voices Beyond."

"Understand that once we reach the Baccata Place, you may not speak."

"We abide by the will of the Voices Beyond."

Dominique bobbed his head. Silence would not be a problem. Hunger, though, was something else. His mother had fed him well with thick tonneck stew and her finest tembeh and wild oat bread, but the thought of not eating until the following evening was enough to make his stomach tighten.

"You know the laws of Stories from Beyond. At the telling fire tomorrow night you may not tell Stories you have told before. You may not tell Stories you have heard from other men and boys."

Protector Bertolescu held his torch over Dominique's head. "And you may not tell the stories of Tara, for those are the tales of women."

Feltham's snigger was cut short when another boy jabbed him in the ribs.

"Feltham?"

"Yes, sir?"

"Share with us the true nature of Stories from Beyond."

"At the ceremony, a man shall tell only a Story that comes directly from the place Beyond, from the place of Absolute Truth."

The boys began to chant.

I shall tell my Story and only my Story.

I shall speak Truth and only my Truth.
And in my words my people shall take comfort.

Dominique's lips moved, but the words were scarcely louder than a whisper.

"Understanding has been reached," Bertolescu said, his head tipped up to the sky.

"So the time has come for these boys to begin their fasting. I plead on their behalf for your blessing, oh, Masters from Beyond."

With a flourish, Bertolescu jabbed the torch into the ground and turned his back to the light. He strode across the circle and led the boys between his hut and that of the Kendako family. Their youngest son, Botta, was third in line behind the Protector.

Once past the line of huts, the darkness closed in on the little group and they bunched up until each boy was close behind the boy in front of him.

"Don't push." Dominique braced against another shove from behind. Feltham, though only a few months older, stood a full head taller.

"If you moved faster than one of Gellebem's snails I wouldn't have to push you, would I?"

"It's his tunic," one of the other boys said, and in the dark, Dominique felt his cheeks flush. His too-long garment twisted around his knees and he stumbled. Feltham had no problem walking in the dark. His ceremonial tunic, inherited from his father and grandfather and great-grandfather and who knows how many fathers before that, was just the right length.

"Boys. Silence during the march."

Heavy clouds obscured even the thin sliver of

moon, so Protector Bertolescu didn't see the next push, one hard enough to send Dominique sprawling in the dirt.

"Someone tripped, sir," said Feltham. "I think it was Dominique."

Dominique could just imagine Feltham's smirk. As if he didn't know exactly who had crashed to the ground.

"Halt." Bertolescu's deep voice brought all the boys to attention, even though they couldn't see any more than the vaguest shadowy form at the head of the line. "Dominique?"

"Yes, sir?"

"Stand."

"I am, sir. Standing, I mean. I got up already."

"May we proceed, then? Unless someone is having a problem and cannot continue?"

If only it were light he'd be able to read the expression on the Protector's face. Was this an invitation to stop or challenge to continue?

The chill breeze bit at Dominique's skinned palms. He barely noticed the sting as he brushed away the hot tears splashing over his cheeks and tried to still the wild beat of terror in his chest. He thought of the warmth of his mother's hut. A wave of nausea threatened to drive him to his knees.

"No, sir," he said, his voice thin and weak. "There is no need to stop. In the name of the Beginning, the Middle, and the End, we may continue."

"Very well. Walk on, boys. The Baccata Place is not far now."

CHAPTER

7

THE BACCATA PLACE

On top of Grace Mountain, Astor drew back the flap of skin on his stomach and watched as three snakes emerged.

As the seven boys shuffled along the path, their eyes adjusted to the dark. All around them, hills rolled skywards, round-shouldered lumps like great sleeping animals protecting the ceremonial encampment in the grove of aspens below.

Darker strips of pine forest swept up and over some of the silent forms while other hills were bare. Here and there, outcroppings of great boulders speared up against the blue-black sky. Low clouds scudded before the wind and Dominique shivered. If it rained, as it so often did at the time of the spring equinox, they would get soaked. The Baccata Place had no roof.

"Prepare for entry."

The little group huddled at the entrance to the sacred hut. Dominique shifted uneasily from foot to foot, waiting for his turn to be blessed.

"Feltham Tomonok. Welcome to Farewell. You enter this place a boy and emerge a man, ready to tell."

Standing in the arched doorway of the small hut, Feltham touched his Namingstone to his lips.

A gust of wind shook the fragile structure. The bamboo framework heaved and sighed. Feltham bowed and then asked, "Might this be my final entry as boy?"

"Do you speak Truth?"

"As ever and always."

"Uphold goodness?"

"As befits an Estorian."

"And how will you begin?"

"As always I will end—with the Truth as I hear it."

"Then enter the silence within—that you may listen, listen."

Feltham ducked into the hut. One by one, each boy stepped forward and the ritual was repeated until only Dominique remained.

"Dominique? You may step forward."

Dominique hesitated. Beyond the Protector, the inside of the hut was dark and silent. A blast of wind whipped his feather tunic around his legs. The Baccata Place, made of supple yew branches interlaced through the bamboo framework, hissed and whispered.

"Dominique?"

Dominique's right hand moved to the pouch at

the waist of his underleggings. Navina's soft bulge gave him little comfort. She stirred in her sleep and protectively he cupped his hand over her. He raised his Namingstone and pressed it to his lips. Its rough face was still warm from being carried close to his body.

"Might this be my final entry as boy?" Dominique dragged the words out from deep inside, forcing them through the silence.

"Do you speak Truth?"

"As ever and always."

Man and boy repeated the chanted words. "Go, then, Dominique. The time has come."

Caught in the doorway, Dominique felt suspended in time, as if he were about to leave the last safe moment in his life. Before him, the Baccata Place trembled before the wind.

"Go. Now."

Dominique held his breath, ducked his head, and stepped into the hut to take his place with the others. He crawled across the dirt floor, avoiding legs and feet, his tunic flapping against the backs of his thighs.

The shapes of the other boys seemed flat against the woven walls as he made his way past them to a spot in the back. Chilly gusts buffeted the fragile shelter as Dominique turned and pressed himself against the wall. He looked up through the open roof, left unfinished so there would be no barrier between the boys and the Stories from Beyond.

There was no sound now from the others. Dominique guessed they, too, were gazing skyward, staring into the rising storm, waiting for their Stories to arrive.

Once settled, Dominique listened for sounds beyond the walls, but Roman Bertolescu's heavy footsteps had already retreated back along the path towards the encampment where dozens of Estorian clans had gathered.

For the rest of that night, and for all the next day until darkness fell again, the boys would fast in silence, waiting to welcome the precious Stories from Beyond. Dominique thought about how their mothers, sisters and aunts, their uncles and the grannies would be preparing for the feasting and celebrations, getting ready for the boys' ceremony.

The women would be filling willow baskets with strips of spiced tangberry leather, stirring slow simmering cauldrons of creamed pelecorn soup, and sweeping the fire circle clean with blessed switch brooms. Uncle Sethka, already back from Corposcia, would be adding the string of beads to the end of Dominique's story stick, the stick his father should have made for him.

Each gathered clan would be completing similar preparations as their twelve-year-old boys waited in huts dotted evenly beyond the perimeter of the encampment. The next night, one group of boys at a time would be brought to the fire. There they would formally present new Stories heard during the long night and day spent in isolation in each group's Baccata Place.

Finally, dawn eased back the darkness and Dominique closed his eyes, willing the stiffness and the cold from his aching legs. Back at the encampment, the men and younger boys would now be oiling the drums and streaking their heavy dance masks with red mud from the Blood River. Inside the Protector's hut, Bertolescu and the grandfathers would begin their meditations with the arrival of first light.

Dominique shifted slightly when he felt Navina move against his side. As the sun rose, she flew from the hut, coming and going for the rest of the day. It was hard not to smile when Feltham pretended to ignore the glorious bird. The boy's mouth tightened and he closed his eyes or looked away whenever Navina swooped into the hut to settle on Dominique's shoulder. His fascination with the kasyapa bird, like that of all the clan members, was impossible to disguise.

Dominique found no comfort in the reprieve granted by the other boys. The only reason they weren't tormenting him now was evident in the looks of scorn and pity they sent his way, if they bothered to look at him at all. Whatever punishment awaited Dominique if he failed to hear a Story was far, far worse than any teasing they might inflict upon him there in the sacred hut.

As the hours passed, whispers began to hiss all around Dominique, filling the small space and rising skyward. Every boy's lips moved with rapid twitches as he heard, shaped, and perfected a Story bestowed on him from Beyond. Dominique pressed his hands over his ears and leaned back against the flexing wall of the hut. His lips remained perfectly still.

8

THE FIRE CIRCLE

*Of the three brothers, only Sontina, the
youngest, was brave enough to step forward
and speak his mind before the king. Alas, the
goblin, Maleshka, had neglected to tell him that
the first to speak always paid for the pleasure
with a visit to the guillotine.*

"Come."

Dominique's head snapped up. How could he
have fallen asleep? He touched the pocket at his
side and felt Navina's still form.

Darkness had fallen again and Dominique
listened as the boys stirred and stretched and
moved towards the doorway. Dominique's heart
thudded as he scrambled outside to join the others.
The waiting was finally over.

The Protector said nothing more. He moved back
along the trail they had travelled the night before.

Dominique stepped carefully, afraid he would stumble and fall. Light-headed from lack of food, and weak with cold and dread, he did not trust his own feet.

He was as prepared as he could be. His heart was open to the Truth. He had found stillness and calm in the Baccata Place. If he could just hold on to the quiet, a Story would enter him when he needed it. The Grand Tellers from Beyond would not let him down. Dominique swallowed again and again, though his mouth was dry. It would be over soon—one way or another. *A Story will come,* he reassured himself, until a soft hoot from a stand of tullah trees startled him. Should he run off? Hide?

Tears rose in his eyes and he forced himself to see another picture in his mind. Dominique stood tall and threw his shoulders back. He would stand proudly with the other boys in front of the fire. There, before his mother, his aunts, all the gathered Estorians, he would open his mouth and the words would come tumbling out. He, too, would raise his new story stick and walk away from the fire circle with the rest of the men. A Story would come to him when he needed it to come.

"Wait."

The boys stopped just beyond the circle of gathered people.

"I bring before you this group of boys, ready to speak, ready to join the ranks of men."

A low rumble answered, "So we may listen, listen."

"Enter the circle."

The boys marched solemnly between clan members, who stepped aside to let them pass.

"That's far enough."

The boys stopped and turned to face Roman Bertolescu. Dominique felt the boys on either side of him tense.

"Dominique Elnedo. Please step forward."

Me? Why me? Why do I have to go first? Dominique wondered, his heart beating wildly.

His knees barely able to support him, Dominique stepped forward, obedient and quiet. He moved from his place among the boys until he stood alone in front of Roman Bertolescu. The clan members leaned in towards the fire, listening.

Dominique shuddered. The great emptiness inside him swelled with each quivery breath, until an ominous darkness, hollow and threatening, filled the silences in his head.

A spray of sparks exploded out of the fire and Dominique flinched. He forced himself to stand still, to fight for calm as Protector Bertolescu solemnly draped a long, feathered cape over his shoulders.

"Look up," the Protector said. Dominique craned his neck and watched the spiral dance of the sparks across the pitch-black night sky. Bertolescu fastened the leather ties under Dominique's chin. His voice softened when he asked, "Are you ready?"

Dominique licked his lips, but he didn't answer. He couldn't. In her hidden pocket, Navina trembled. To calm her, Dominique gently smoothed the feathers on the back of the little bird's neck. As his thumb rubbed back and forth, she settled deeper into her pouch and his own breathing slowed.

The Protector backed away and spoke a few quiet words to the waiting drummers. Dominique stood alone before the fire, unable to enjoy its warmth. The drums began to sing softly, slowly. *The Story will come*, he told himself again. It *had* to come. No boy remained silent once the drummers began to call the Stories down.

With a wide sweep of his arms, Roman Bertolescu signalled for the masked drummers to speed up. The rhythmic *pat-pat-a-pat-pat-a* grew faster and louder. The ceremonial masks, painted in black, yellow, and red, bobbed from side to side. Framed by wild halos of black hair, the faces of the drumming figures with their hooked beak noses and gaping mouths were terrifying and beautiful.

Dominique tore his gaze away and watched the Protector raise his palms to the sky. His long robes billowed behind him as he made the gesture. "Oh, Great Keepers of Stories, we stand before you meek and obedient." The drums pounded louder. "We honour your wisdom, your generosity, your power."

The Protector touched Dominique lightly on the forehead with his sacred bone-handled story stick.

"This boy, Dominique Elnedo, listens with a clear mind and an open heart."

The great figure towered over the boy, his face licked by shadows, his arms once again sweeping upwards. "Oh, Masters of Story, send the Stories down!"

Pounding wildly on the drums, the masked

Estorians grunted and howled.

All his life Dominique had seen Bertolescu's strong arms embrace the messages from Beyond. So many boys had stood in this very place before the Protector, draped in the feather cape, empty bellies aching, hearts racing. Now Dominique was one of them and all he felt was a bitter sickness eating into his stomach.

Bertolescu turned once to the east and once to the west, each time spreading his fingers and then closing them in tight fists as if grasping at invisible strings suspended in the air. His whole body jerked as the drumbeats pummelled him.

The Protector turned back to Dominique and touched his head, shoulders, chest, and back with the sacred story stick. All the while he chanted,

From the place Beyond,
the Stories call—listen, listen.
Words gather,
turn, and fall—listen, listen.
Whispers enter the ready heart
and so the Stories form—listen, listen.
So you may speak,
so you may tell,
and we may listen, listen.

With each familiar phrase, the hollow pit in Dominique's stomach deepened. He felt no different than he ever had. When would he hear it? When would the Voices from Beyond speak to him? He listened hard, strained to catch a whisper, anything, any kind of beginning. Blood rushed through his ears, echoing the relentless thumping of the drums.

Crona, hunched and crooked, took the story stick from Protector Bertolescu and the leader turned his back on Dominique. This was the moment the Story would begin to bubble up, its arrival signalled by twitching lips and shudders that would shake his body. His arms might flail, he might fall to the ground or leap in circles, shouting. Dominique had seen many boys as they prepared to speak and it was always thrilling.

The women and girls began to chant and dance, their bare feet sending up soft poofs of dirt as they stamped, step-step-hop-step-step, around the circle in time to the beating drums. Their arms rose and fell and with every other step-hop they clapped a double handclap—first high above their heads, then low on one side, then low on the other.

And so you speak
and so you tell,
so we may listen, listen.

All the Estorians sang together to the wise Masters Beyond, calling the Stories down to the boy beside the fire. Despite his mounting panic, Dominique began to sway, caught in the powerful rhythms, responding to the will of his people. He moved to the *pa-da-thump-pa-da-thump* of the drums, his body clapping and stamping as if it didn't belong to him. His head filled with the unavoidable thumping progress of time, each drumbeat another second lost.

The Protector repeated the incantation.

And so you tell,
so we may listen, listen. . . .

He repeated it once, twice, three times as the dancers moved faster, faster in an ever-tightening circle.

"The Story is coming *now*," Dominique repeated under his breath. *I will speak so they may listen, listen.*

Fragments of tales flitted through his mind. But the only ones that held still long enough for him to recognize were pieces of the Tara stories. *Tara's women wove strong nets from their long, black hair. . . .* No good. The Earth Goddess stories were women's stories. *And when they cast their nets into the night sky, the stars were caught.* If he told the star story, or any Tara legend, he would be ridiculed, or worse. Beaten, maybe. *And so, the Estorian people came to have fire. Each woman took a star and used its brightness to bring warmth and comfort to her children.* He didn't dare think of what punishment might befall him if he, a boy, at the boys' Coming of Stories, uttered the tales of women.

Dominique tried to hold his mind clear and empty so a proper man's Story could make itself known, but the only words that came to him were the endless, repeating litany, *the Story must come, the Story must come,* hammering inside his head with each drumbeat, with each shout from the dancers, each agonized thud of his flailing heart.

When the fire popped and the sparks flew, it was the stars trying to return to their homes in the sky.

The smallest girl, Tiki, spiralled in towards the fire. The young girls followed her so that now there were two rings of dancers—the young girls in a circle close to Dominique and the fire, and the older girls and women on the outside circle, whirling and leaping in the opposite direction. Beyond them, another, smaller fire crackled behind the grannies. They huddled together to keep away the chill of the spring night air, cradling the clan infants still too young to take part in the ceremony.

The other boys had moved back, out of the way of the dancers. They waited in the shadows beyond the edge of the second fire. Before long, each, in turn, would stand before Protector Bertolescu. Each would share the Story he had received from the Masters Beyond.

The Story will come. Dominique swayed more quickly as the chanting, drumming, clapping, and stamping sped up and grew louder.

Protector Bertolescu backed away and passed between the women. As if responding to some silent signal, everyone suddenly stopped. Where only a moment before the air had rung with the shouts and cries of the dancers and drummers, now there was silence as the glittering eyes of the gathered Estorian people turned to Dominique.

The boy drew a breath and raised his arms skyward. The long feather cloak swayed slightly and the whole crowd leaned in closer—listening, listening.

Dominique made his mind empty and still as he had been taught. *Now,* he thought. He closed his eyes and lowered his arms. Bitter helplessness squeezed inside his chest. The Masters of Story had failed him. Or—and the thought made his empty stomach heave—he had failed the Masters.

Navina stirred and he slipped his hand into the hidden pouch to quiet her. The tip of her hooked beak nibbled gently at the side of his thumb. A whirl of random phrases made clear thought impossible.

The curse of the Silencers fell like a dark blanket over the sleeping children. . . . Tara understood even the cries of the wind. . . . When the great beast roared, the boy, Tonio, let fly the stone. . . .

Fragments of the Tara stories mixed with pieces of the historical stories. Tara's net ensnared great kings. Battles, plagues, and pirates joined the muddle with images of Dominique's past—his father turning to wave from the back of a horse, his mother clutching his hand the day Dominique became lost at the market in Feremeos, the day he found Navina.

"Dominique?"

The boy looked up at the Protector. His mouth was so dry he feared that even if, by some miracle, words would come to him, he would not be able to speak them. Oh, his head was filled with stories all right, but they were stories he had heard all his life. Nothing was new. With a gasp of grief, he acknowledged the hideous truth. He swayed, weakened from the lack of food, from the strain of waiting, faint with the knowledge that he, Dominique Elnedo, had no Story to tell.

9

BANISHED

When night was blackest, the Silencers descended into the dreams of the sleeping children.

With a voice that was scarcely louder than a whisper, Dominique said, "I have no Story."

Gasps rippled through the crowd.

Dominique had never known such pure, ice-cold terror. Everything he had ever understood was blanked out. The faces around him were rigid, uncomprehending. Men peeled off their masks. His words, admitting failure, had been spilled among his people. As much as he would have loved to take them back and offer something else, something better, he could not. His knees buckled and he sank slowly to the ground. Bertolescu did not step forward to break the boy's fall. The Protector's hands remained limp at his sides.

Beyond understanding and stiff with fear,

Dominique fell forward until his head touched the ground. There, he waited. Sharp gravel bit into his forehead but he dared not move. Disturbed by the sudden fall, Navina squirmed in his pocket. Dominique summoned all his willpower and shifted slightly so she would not be crushed against his side. He held his breath and the bird settled. He waited to hear what his punishment would be.

All around him Dominique's people shifted and murmured. The uneasy swell of horrified whispers grew louder.

"No Story?"

"But what will happen?"

"Impossible."

"Punished?"

And then, a familiar, beautiful voice rose above the general murmuring of the others.

"Dominique—my baby! Please! Get up and speak!"

Dominique remained where he was, paralyzed. He heard his aunts trying to calm his mother but she would not be quiet. "Speak! Say anything! You *must* have a Story."

"Dania. Shh, the Protector is going to speak."

If only he could jump up and run to comfort his mother, to feel her protective arms around him. But Dominique lay as if slain, waiting on the ground to hear what his fate would be. The cold numbed his knees, seeped into the palm of his left hand, the delicate warmth of his bird cradled in the other. The prickle of gravel was so sharp against his forehead he had to bite the inside of his cheek so he didn't cry out with the pain of it.

Total silence descended over the watchers again as Dominique heard the heavy sound of Protector Bertolescu's footfall beside him.

"Estorian law is quite clear on the matter of the Voiceless," the Protector began. *The curse of the Silencers fell like a dark blanket over the sleeping children. . . .*

Dania's weeping was a wave of agony washing over all of them, chilling Dominique to the bone.

"We, the men of the Estorian people, are the keepers of Truth, the holders of great Stories. We, alone, are blessed with the ability to hear Stories from the Masters Beyond."

Mutters of "Ah, yes!" rose from the crowd. Someone began to chant, "So we may tell, so we may listen," until Bertolescu had to clear his throat and demand silence. All but Dominique's mother complied. Her inconsolable weeping continued when the Protector went on. "This boy has been silenced. In his silence we find the embodiment of evil and weakness. Without the ability to hear and then share the great Stories from Beyond, we have no purpose. This boy has no purpose."

"Please, no—his father will return to—"

Whatever his mother was about to say was cut off by the aunts' hushing and comforting.

In his folded position on the ground, Dominique wept. The jubilant excitement of the crowd had completely evaporated. With each word Bertolescu spoke, with each of his mother's heart-rending wails, with each subdued chant of "So we may listen," the mood blackened.

Protector Bertolescu spoke again.

"This boy has failed all of us. This boy must be punished."

Dominique sucked in his lower lip and clamped it hard between his teeth. A yearning bigger than he was pushed all rational thought from his mind. He wished, more than anything, that he could just stand up, turn to the crowd, and speak with the wisdom and grace they expected. Why couldn't he find the words that would make them listen with intense, total concentration, as all other Estorian men were able to do?

But he had no opportunity to move, no second chance to redeem himself because the Protector was speaking again.

"A life without purpose is no life."

"Please have mercy! He is just a boy!"

It sounded as if the Protector was about to pronounce a death sentence and a total, momentary calm washed over Dominique. So, he was to die and then his suffering would at least be over. Then his thoughts started moving so quickly he could hardly follow them. Would the end come quickly? How was he to die? With a quick stroke of the blade across the back of his neck like a tonneck?

Dominique pressed closer to the earth, his heart wild and alive again. It hammered at his tunic and hot tears flowed freely down his cheeks.

"In a moment, the way of the Grand Tellers Beyond will be revealed to me." Bertolescu began to chant, calling down a message, some direction for a sentence appropriate for Dominique's crime of silence.

"His father came to us, after all!" Dania pleaded. Desperate to intervene, her words poured out, loud and intense, drowning out shocked gasps and horrified hushing. "His father needed time to come to the Truth. Perhaps it will be the same for his son?"

This comment made the Protector pause in his chanting. When he spoke again he sounded a little gentler, almost forgiving. Dominique puzzled over his mother's words. What did she mean that his father had needed time to come to the Truth? According to the Tara stories, the Truth came to a boy when he was ready to receive it—not the other way around. And why did she keep talking about his father, he wondered? That man, that stranger, was no father if he could not even be bothered to witness his son's execution.

A tumble of images clashed together in Dominique's head: Boris Elnedo astride a grey horse at the head of a group of riders; Boris Elnedo waving to Dominique and his mother—"To the Lord of Grenille and beyond!"; Dominique, choking on tears, knowing it wasn't right to be sad, not right to hold back the man of the family when he leaves on an expedition for telling. Dominique, grabbing at his mother's hand.

He will be back, little one.

But when? But when?

Your father is one of the great travellers. One of the great tellers. You must be proud of him and never feel sad during his absences.

For a crazed moment, Dominique imagined that *now* was the time his father would come back. He would know that tonight was the night his son was supposed to tell a Story of his own. But of course, when a man's voice spoke, it was not that of his father. It was Protector Bertolescu.

"You shall have a year and a day to find your voice."

A new tangle of questions cluttered Dominique's mind. A reprieve? He was not to be killed on the spot? What *did* his mother mean about his father? His father came from where? A year and a day? He had a year and a day to find a Story? Dominique could not wait to run to his mother's arms, to feel her warm embrace and hear her soothing whispers in his ear.

His hope faded quickly when Bertolescu continued, "This is not easy for me to say, Dania. I do not know how this has happened, but the boy, Dominique, is clearly cursed. He may contaminate the others if he stays. For the good of our people he must leave."

Dominique could hardly breathe.

Bertolescu straightened up and spoke loudly and clearly to his gathered people. "This boy, Dominique, son of Dania and Boris Elnedo, must be banished for the period of one year and one day. During his time of banishment he may have no contact with any Estorian, and no Estorian may assist him in any way. At the end of his time of exile he may return to this fire circle to speak. Should he still be silent, he shall, at that moment, and without further reprieve, be executed."

Dominique's mother wailed, a long, shrieking cry of grief and shock. The Protector's hands touched the back of Dominique's head, indicating the boy was to get up.

Numb, weeping, Dominique stood. The old Estorian leader lifted the boy's chin, undid the leather thongs, and removed the feather cape.

"But, wh-where shall I go?"

"Think of the story of the boy Tibor."

Tibor. The boy whose voice was stolen by Silencers. Because Tibor could not speak, he could not tell Stories and because he could not tell Stories, he was banished from his clan. The Tibor story was told to children who didn't tell as many Stories as they should. Dominique had heard the horrifying tale many, many times. In his worst dreams he had never imagined such a thing could really happen.

"Go where he goes," the Protector said.

To the Cave of Departure? There really was such a place?

Protector Bertolescu took his hand from Dominique's shoulder and turned away. At first, the place where Bertolescu's hand had rested burned red hot and then, as he walked away, the invisible imprint grew ice cold.

"No!"

Dominique sprinted from the fire, pushing through the wall of people. "Mama!"

"Let me hold him!" Dania cried, pulling free from her sisters and rushing to her only son.

They threw their arms around each other, clinging fiercely in the darkness. Ahh, her smell, her warmth, her closeness! Dania's body shook with sobs but her arms around him were strong.

"What's that?"

He lifted his head from her breast, listening to the strange hissing sound swirling all around them. The clan members surrounded mother and son, not touching, not moving, but hissing.

Dania's breath caught, a sob half strangled in her throat. The hissing was loud and terrifying, like an insistent wind tearing them apart.

Dania's arms loosened and dropped to her sides.

"Mama . . ." Dominique said, softly. But nobody answered.

Dania's sisters and the other women flanked her, turned her from her child.

"No!"

But it was too late.

"Come, Dania," Crona said. "No good could come of this boy . . . not without a father to bless him on this day."

Dania sobbed, heartbroken.

"It's best you leave him," Crona added. Though Dania wailed, she did not struggle as they led her away.

The others, too, turned their backs on Dominique. The hissing stopped. Then his family, his clan, his people melted away, back towards the circle of huts hunched against him.

CHAPTER
10

TRAVEL EAST

*With the words of the warrior lord ringing in
his ears, Tibor turned
and faced east. Alone, he began to walk
towards the Misty Mountains.*

Dominique hesitated by the fire. Tibor and the
Silencers? It couldn't really happen like that, could
it? And as for the Cave of Departure, surely the
magical cave was a made-up place, not somewhere
that real boys went.

Deep within the cave, Tibor found his voice.

The Protector couldn't mean that Dominique
should just walk off into the night without food,
completely alone! Dominique peered into the darkness beyond the circle of firelight where his people
had disappeared, but nothing moved in the shadows.
Closing his eyes, Dominique tried to remember
exactly what the story said about getting to the cave.

Tibor turned and faced east.

East? Dominique swallowed hard at the thought of travelling toward the rising sun. Everyone knew the eastern highlands were filled with strange and dangerous creatures. It was better to stay far, far from the highlands. If you had a choice, that is.

"Hello? Are you there?" he called out to the spaces between the trees where his clan had vanished. If only he had seen a banishment before. Did they really expect him to just turn and go? Now? What if he didn't do it? What if he just refused to move? Had anyone ever returned from exile? Not the boy Tibor.

Tibor was never seen again. Some say he fought a vicious battle with a leranon at the top of a cliff high in the Misty Mountains and disappeared.

Sniffling, Dominique backed away from the fire. Wisps and shreds of the women's stories he had heard all his life mixed in a wild confusion in his head.

Tara rose in the darkness and lit the fire in the sky.

Dominique spun around.

"Mama?" He coughed and moved away from the smoke.

Tara's tribe of maidens tended the fire, spinning night into day.

Dominique pressed his eyes shut and listened to the diminishing echoes of his mother's resonant voice. He shuddered, remembering the way she made the different voices of the maidens as she told the Estorian people when the seasons were about to change and when it was time to travel to a new camp; the way she sang the old songs of how the creatures came to be.

When the Earth Goddess, Tara, first left her cave, the darkness pressed upon her. She tried to breathe fire into the sky so all the creatures might see, the crops would grow, and the Estorians would prosper, but the effort exhausted her and she had to retreat to her cave for one hundred years.

His lips moved as he whispered the familiar words to the abandoned fire circle. If only he had been born a girl, the Tara stories would have been enough. Telling the story of how Tara and her maidens had captured the sun would have saved him.

I have a year and a day, he reasoned. But immediately, darker thoughts drowned out the timid voice of reassurance. Even if he returned to the fire after his time of exile, if he still had not heard the Stories he was meant to hear, he would be as dead as the warrior king Slorian, who died on the horns of a crazed bull during competition at the Coliseum in Carnillo.

Dominique shook his head. He tried to push away the stories of people coming to hideous ends. But there were so many of them! There was Althazar, the shepherd who had refused to sell his only daughter, Velya, to the miller, Globeschin. Althazar had been ground into dust between Globeschin's massive millstones. Althazar's daughter hadn't fared much better. After her father's demise, she had been so sick with grief she had eaten three handfuls of deep purple sythlyx berries.

Velya lay writhing on the ground for thirty-seven hours before, finally, she crossed the Jade Bridge and found peace in death. Not, however, before seven ravens had fought in the skies above for the honour of plucking out her eyeballs. *The maiden's body was so full of sythlyx poison that after the strongest raven snapped up the eyeballs of the fallen girl, the bird dropped from the sky like a stone.*

Dominique had heard so many death stories, he knew that no matter how grisly the end might be, beyond the Jade Bridge was a peaceful and gentle place. Even so, he was in no hurry to join the eternal circle of Grand Tellers. With his luck, the Grand Tellers of Beyond wouldn't even want him and his non-existent voice. Then where would he go?

A gust of wind swirled around his bare arms. He wore only his ceremonial tunic and his thin cotton underleggings. He tugged the bottom edge of the garment down over his knees, but it wasn't really thick enough to protect him from the chilly air. Dominique drew a long, hiccuping breath.

Due east. As far as the tusk on Rain Mountain. Then Tibor followed the sound of falling water.

Dominique didn't know what else to do. He chose that single thread in the thickly woven fabric of the thousands and thousands of stories he had heard his whole life. He picked up the thread and repeated it over and over again as he turned away from the fire and began to walk.

11

THE ASPEN WOODS

*And so Tibor walked due east, as far as the tusk
on Rain Mountain.*

Dominique walked as slowly as he could, but it
wasn't long before he had crossed to the far edge
of the wide clearing in the Aspen Woods. When he
reached the trees, he hesitated and turned to look
back.

The flickering fire spilled into the clearing,
casting a golden pool of light. As Dominique
watched, he saw figures begin to shift and move,
blocking and revealing the dancing flames beyond.
The others had returned.

Steady thumps drifted towards him and he realized with a start the men were drumming. The boys'
ceremony was beginning again without him. His
throat tightened and he clutched the silvery-grey
trunk of a young aspen to steady himself.

Another boy might fail. If someone else—Zeb, or Marcus, or maybe Feltham—came this way, too, he might have company as he journeyed to the Cave of Departure.

Dominique waited a long time at the edge of the Aspen Woods, just in case he was not the only one. He stood in silence, his hand cupped lightly around the warm fluff of his sleeping bird.

But nobody came. After many hours, the distant drumming stopped, the figures disappeared, and the fire died away until all that remained was a dull glow. Reluctantly, Dominique turned and looked once again to the east. Already the horizon glowed through the trees with a suggestion of greyness slightly lighter than the total darkness behind him.

Stiff, cold, hungry, and not quite sure where he was going, Dominique headed off into the trees.

By mid-morning the sun was high enough and warm enough to make the going uncomfortable, even in the dappled shade of the woods. The cere- monial tunic he wore was made of coarse wool and decorated with thousands and thousands of feathers. Each year the grannies checked the tunics to make sure all the feathers were securely fastened. They poked any loose quill ends through the rough woven fabric and then fastened them in place with a daub of sticky tar from the Black River.

The ceremonial tunics were meant to be worn only during the preparations in the Baccata Place and the ceremony that followed. Now, as Dominique followed the path through the ghostly white aspen trunks, his skin prickled and burned from the constant rubbing of the feather ends.

"Hop off, Navina," he said, nudging his bird from her perch on his shoulder. She ruffled her feathers and lifted first one foot and then the other. Ever since she had emerged from the close darkness of Dominique's pocket, she had been uneasy, wary of flying off in unfamiliar territory.

"Hurry up, silly. I have to get this itchy thing off." He spoke boldly, as if a loud voice could defeat the stillness around him.

Still Navina refused to move.

"Here. Hop up." He pressed his finger against her chest and she stepped onto his hand. His voice sounded strange, dwarfed by the towering trees, but he pushed the words out anyway. "Sit up there for a minute."

Dominique placed Navina on a branch at the side of the path and she raised her crest in alarm at being forced to sit alone.

"I won't leave you there. Don't worry."

Dominique glanced down at his cotton under-leggings and then at the bird who watched everything he did with bright interest.

"Don't laugh."

Navina didn't laugh, but she did let out a piercing whistle as he pulled his tunic up over his head and bundled it in his arms. "Come on. Let's go."

Navina hopped off the branch with a blue-green flutter and landed on Dominique's head. Her sharp claws prickled lightly on his scalp as she clutched at his hair to balance herself when he moved on once again.

Just carrying the tunic was miserable. Wherever the feathers touched his already irritated skin, Dominique felt prickly and itchy. Holding the annoying article of clothing away from his body only made his arms and shoulders ache. To make matters worse, Dominique's stomach was completely empty, and he was so tired he stumbled and lurched. "Sorry!" he said after a particularly awkward misstep sent Navina fluttering and squawking in protest.

Stupid Bertolescu, he caught himself thinking. How could the Protector have sent him off without instructions, without a map, without any help at all? What did he expect Dominique to do?

Dominique tripped over a tree root and flung his hands out to catch himself. Navina squawked. Was he supposed to turn back and beg for forgiveness? Keep going? What if he couldn't find the cave? Dominique walked on and on but all he saw was more trees, trunks straight and white, slivers of bark peeling like crispy skin to reveal black wounds beneath. A cave? This was not the kind of place where one would find a cave.

Dominique's ankle twisted when he stepped awkwardly into a hollow on the trail and he fell to his knees. "Fen-wah!" he swore and then looked guiltily behind him to see who might have heard. There was nothing there but the endless rows of the absolutely straight aspen trees. No, he could not, would not go a single step farther.

A light breeze rippled through the first green leaves of spring, and a pair of small, brown birds flitted lightly from branch to branch before disappearing deeper into the forest. Dominique rose slowly to his feet as Navina peeped and twittered, mimicking her wild cousins.

"Fen-wah!" Dominique shouted the swear word at the trees. "Fen-waaaaaaaah!"

The only answer was the ripple of a breeze tickling the leaves. Dominique sighed and turned back to face the direction they had been travelling.

"Aggh!" he shrieked.

"Hoy, traveller," the old woman said.

Dominique flushed deep crimson. "Ahhhh . . . excuse me. Pardon me. . . ." Warily, he watched the woman who stood right in front of him, not an arm's length away. Where on earth had she come from? She was tall, taller than he was, but as stooped and ancient as any of the grannies. The creases in her skin were deep and overlapped, one set of lines running into another as if a giant hand had reached out and squeezed her face into a series of interlocking fissures and cracks.

Her head was completely bald and at each temple a smear of red colour stood out against her weathered brown skin. She rested on a gnarled walking stick and studied Dominique with a pair of shiny black eyes that seemed much too small for her face, set deeply, as they were, into her wrinkles.

"You look a sight, you do," she said.

Dominique looked down at his bare torso and felt his blush deepen. He was covered with red welts and splotches from where the feather tips had rubbed and poked him.

"Come," the woman said, and she slipped away, not along the main trail, but onto a small path leading off to one side.

If Dominique had not been so tired, or if he had had a weapon, or even if he had been clothed properly, he might have considered arguing. One did not follow complete strangers off into the forest. As it was, he didn't feel he had any choice but to follow the crone wherever she might lead him. Maybe she would know whether he was heading in the general direction of the Cave of Departure.

Dominique was relieved he had to do no more than stay upright and keep one foot moving after the other, carefully following the swish and sway of the old woman's heavy, black skirts. Her feet, swaddled in strips of soft leather, moved silently through the woods, sure of the way. Dominique felt like a great oaf by comparison as he tripped and fumbled, breaking twigs underfoot and making enough noise to wake the dead.

The old woman said nothing, never looking back to see how he was doing. *She doesn't need to,* he thought bitterly. With all the noise he was making it would be pretty obvious if he fell behind.

They walked on, moving deeper into the woods and farther from the main trail, ducking under low branches and squeezing around prickly wattle spear bushes.

"Don't step in the roughweed," the crone said, indicating a patch of bright yellow leaves with her walking stick. "You'll get boils."

When she stopped at the edge of a small clearing, Dominique was so busy concentrating on not falling over that he bumped right into her broad backside.

"Oh, excuse me!"

Navina fluttered into the air and then landed on Dominique's shoulder. He winced as her sharp claws pinched his inflamed skin.

The old crone stepped to the side. A small house in front of them nestled into the surrounding trees. Two twisted trees in large wooden tubs stood guard on either side of a bright blue door.

The door seemed too small for the old woman, and sure enough, when she pushed it open, she had to duck so she didn't bump her head on the door jamb. Dominique hesitated at the threshold.

"Come in, my boy. The soup is good, and ready for the eating."

BREAKING BREAD

*The baby girl wailed and wailed when the
family of foxes dragged her away to their den
in the roots of the ancient oak deep in the
Brinesca Forest.*

"I suppose you two are hungry?" the woman said
once they were inside. She lowered herself onto a
squat stool and poked at the fire crackling in the
hearth. It was the first time she had acknowledged
Navina. She didn't seem to find it strange that
Dominique was travelling with such an unusual
companion.

Dominique didn't answer. He sank onto a pile of
furs where the woman had indicated he should sit.
The minute he stopped moving, he felt like his
body was sinking away from him, the flesh melting
from his bones.

Navina hopped onto the handle of a basket that

stood on the floor nearby and began to preen her long, elegant tail feathers.

Dominique yawned and clapped his hand over his mouth, suddenly shy.

"And tired," the crone continued. "Here. Eat some of this and then sleep. Tell me later where your travels take you."

Dominique took the wooden bowl and sniffed at the steaming soup inside. He dipped the heel of bread she offered into the rich broth.

"Mmmmm," he said, his mouth full.

"Never mind. Just eat," she said. "Here, little one," she said to Navina. "It's just seed and a bit of chicklegrass. Don't look so suspicious."

Navina hopped to the edge of the saucer and pecked warily at the offering. She cocked her head to one side when the old woman offered her an egg cup full of water. She drank, sipping the water and then letting the droplets trickle down her throat.

Dominique gobbled down his meal. He dipped and slurped and sucked the delicious tangy soup from the bread and then tore at the crust with his teeth.

"I'm glad I didn't make that too hot," the woman remarked. "Isn't that right, Vulpescio?"

A red fox stood in the corner where he had been sleeping and bowed deeply. His delicate, pointed snout reached towards Dominique, who pulled his bowl back and watched the handsome animal warily.

Navina let out a sharp whistle and flew straight up to the rafters. She peeped several more high-pitched warnings and huddled back into the corner where the chimney met the ceiling.

"When you're finished, you'd better give him the bowl to lick or he might jump on you," the woman said with a sly grin.

Vulpescio stepped forward and watched intently as Dominique ate. The fox's eyes followed the bread from bowl to mouth and back. Dominique tipped the bowl to his lips and then, not wanting to get too close, thrust the bowl at the delicate animal.

The fox had no interest whatsoever in the boy. Instead, he carefully pressed one paw against the inside of the bowl and tipped it upright so he could lick out the leftovers in comfort.

"So, now you've met my companion, Vulpescio. Perhaps you'd like to tell me your name?"

"Dominique. Dominique Elnedo."

"Elnedo. That's a very old name. Are you a Campriano?"

Dominique shook his head sharply. Most certainly not! "No," he said aloud. "I am an Estorian."

"So you think, so you think."

"Camprianos are liars and cowards and . . ." Dominique stopped. Maybe she had friends who belonged to that other nation of storytellers.

But the woman had eyes only for the fox who, finished with the empty bowl, had moved to a spot on the other end of the bed of furs. Vulpescio turned three times in place, curled into a ball, and relaxed with a sigh.

"My name is Bethusela."

"Bethusela?" He had never heard such a name.

"Bethusela is also a very old name. But, I'm sure such trivial details as the origins of old names would be of no interest to a boy like you. Boring, yes?"

She didn't really seem to expect an answer, so Dominique said nothing. Another yawn crept up on him and he covered his mouth with his hand.

"Yes. It's best you sleep now."

"Here?" Dominique asked, feeling a bit stupid.

Bethusela nodded. "Lie down. Vulpescio will soon be off in the Land of Slumber. You won't be disturbed."

"What about Navina?" The bird watched warily from her high perch.

"She will be all right. After his nap Vulpescio will be going out." She looked sternly at the fox. "Not that you would dream of hurting a house guest, would you?"

The fox raised an eyebrow and looked bored. His nose, however, twitched and quivered and Dominique noticed that the handsome animal kept licking his lips.

Dominique's head bobbed forward involuntarily, and up on her perch Navina gave a soft, worried chirrup.

"My dear boy, you must sleep."

There was no way to resist her command. Dominique slowly tipped over until he lay stretched out on his side, his cheek nestled in the soft pile of furs.

He blinked once, twice, and then he was asleep.

13

EMBELLICA BERRIES AND TEA

*Victorious at last, Lord Andaglio danced atop
the Tower of Roon, threw down his armour,
and spread his arms as though he might soar
free as a bird over his new lands.*

When Dominique awoke some time later, he had
no idea how long he had slept. An indentation in
the fur beyond his feet showed where the fox had
been curled into a tight red ball. But now, Vulpescio
was gone.

"So, you slept well?"

Dominique turned and looked at Bethusela.

"Aggh!"

"Shhh. There's no need to shout."

Dominique stared, horrified and fascinated by
what he saw. The old woman hung upside down
from her ankles. Leather straps around her lower
legs were fastened to two hooks driven into one of

the heavy oak ceiling beams. She was so tall her bald head scarcely cleared the rough dirt floor below. A soft coil of rope around her knees prevented her wide skirts from falling down around her head and engulfing her completely. Navina perched on the old woman's toes, twittering happily to herself.

"What . . . what are you doing?" Dominique managed to ask.

"Thinking."

"Like that?"

"My back pains me, my boy. Hanging like this does wonders."

Her arms flopped loosely at either side of her head. The backs of her hands rested easily on the cottage floor. Her face was bright red, nearly the same shade as the smears she wore on her temples.

Dominique stared, not caring that his gaze might be considered rude. He had never seen anything like it—a woman as old as the grannies dangling from the ceiling. Dominique wondered how on earth Bethusela managed to get herself up into that awkward position.

"Would you like to tell me where you are heading, young man? You hardly seem prepared for a long journey."

For a wild moment, Dominique thought he might just get up, walk out the door of the cottage, and go back to the ceremonial encampment.

Bethusela crossed her arms over her stomach and swung back and forth. In the fire, a log sizzled.

"There's no shame in running away. You would

not be the first boy who squabbled with his mama and set off to make her angry."

Dominique shook his head. She was so, so wrong.

"There is no shame in going home, either."

"Home? I have no home."

Bethusela made a smacking sound with her mouth and her tongue poked in and out, leaving moist shiny spots on her lips. She narrowed her eyes. "No home?"

Dominique shook his head.

Bethusela heaved a great sigh. "Off you go," she said to Navina, who hopped off her perch and glided across the room to Dominique's outstretched hand. The crone reached up and pulled on a rope looped over one of the ceiling beams. She hauled herself up until she was folded nearly in half. Then, holding most of her weight with one arm, she loosened the straps around her ankles and let her feet drop to the ground.

When she was upright again, she undid the skirt-holding rope and hooked it over a peg beside the door. Slightly out of breath, she moved over to the fire where she crouched down. Using a long, cast-iron hook, she lifted a boiling kettle from the flames and set it on one of the hearthstones.

The hideousness of the truth was suddenly more than Dominique could stand to admit to himself, never mind to this strange old woman.

"There, now, my boy. No need to cry. I'll make tea."

She bustled about, swearing under her breath as

she struggled with the tight lid of an earthenware pot.

"Ach, clarpen! There we are. I must oil that lid before there's a terrible accident and I spill this everywhere."

Bethusela pulled a pinch of aromatic purple leaves out of the container and dropped them into a heavy iron teapot. She poured hot water over the leaves and then clapped on the lid, capturing the steam inside.

"My heavens, boy! You'll weep your way out to sea, you will! Hush now."

Dominique gritted his teeth and tried to breathe through his nose, but the sobs would not stop. He just sounded more snuffly and felt even more foolish. He could scarcely believe it when he heard himself let out a long, miserable wail.

"Oh, my. Here, suck on one of these." The old woman plucked a withered red fruit from a cluster hanging from the rafters.

Horrified at his outburst, Dominique took the dry fruit from her and looked up through his tears.

"Embellica berries. Take your mind off your troubles for certain."

The last thing he felt like doing was tasting exotic fruit but he felt he owed the woman something a little more polite than more weeping and wailing. Though the skin of the berry looked leathery, between Dominique's fingers it flaked and peeled like old, dry bark.

"Quick. Put it on your tongue. Let the layers melt away."

The twinkle had returned to Bethusela's eyes. "Eeuuch . . ."

The berry fizzled and popped on his tongue.

"Don't spit it out! They're very hard to come by!"

Easy for her to say! She didn't have a sizzling, popping fireball on her tongue!

Dominique was so busy trying to keep his taste buds from leaping out of his mouth, he didn't notice the tears drying on his cheeks.

"You're drooling," Bethusela remarked.

Dominique slurped as he tried to suck back the embarrassing string of spittle. As suddenly as the berry had come to life in his mouth it hissed away to nothing until only a sliver remained, no bigger than a slip of chewed fingernail. This he swallowed and then managed to give Bethusela a little smile as he wiped his chin with the back of his hand.

"So, tell me, right from the start, how you come to be travelling through my woods."

Though his voice was soft, Dominique found he could speak. "My voice was stolen."

"Stolen?" She arched an eyebrow and peered into the teapot.

"By the Silencers."

"Ahh."

"You've heard of them?"

"I've heard stories. Do you remember when it happened?"

"No. I must have been little because I have never heard any Stories from Beyond. Not like the other boys."

"What kind of stories do the other boys tell?"

Bethusela poured the tea and added a little honey to Dominique's cup.

"About all kinds of things. Like I remember Feltham told a Story about a snake when he was about six."

"Snake stories are good stories?"

"Feltham's snake Story was rather good. But the Stories don't have to be about snakes."

"You don't know *any* stories?" Bethusela opened a cupboard and pulled out a sheaf of long, golden grass. She shook it above a shallow dish and seeds spilled from the dry, ripe seed heads. "Golden spirit grass. Good for kasyapa feather colour."

Dominique saw now that Navina's feathers looked a little pale. "Oh, Navina—I'm sorry. I should have . . ." How could he have failed to notice the bird wasn't feeling her best?

"Not to worry. She'll soon perk up. See? She likes the seeds. Now, answer my question."

Dominique had to think for a moment. "Oh . . . I do know some stories—well, lots of them."

"So, you are *not* silent after all?"

"The stories I know are the wrong kind of stories. A boy can't tell a woman's tale . . . or a man's Story he has heard before including the stories from history. At least, not during the Coming of Stories ceremony. After that, it's fine to tell history stories sometimes but not women's stories, not ever." Dominique paused. He had never realized how complicated it must all sound to someone who did not live and die by the art of storytelling. "That's the whole reason we have the boys' Coming of Stories Ceremony where we are supposed to tell special Stories—the ones that come from the Place Beyond."

"So, you are supposed to hear these . . . these special stories at the ceremony?"

Dominique nodded miserably.

"And you didn't hear what you were supposed to hear?"

"No," he said softly.

"Is there no cure for this . . . silence that plagues you?"

Dominique shook his head. "Believe me, my mother tried everything—she used to pack my ears with black lamb's wool soaked in the juice of boiled ash bark and rolled in garlic paste. It smelled bad, but not as rotten as the stuff she smeared behind my ears. That was disgusting."

"I'm sure it was!"

"I even had to stop being with my mother because the other women said I would only learn the Tara stories if I just listened to her. I was about six when she made me spend the days with the other boys so I could have lessons the way I was supposed to."

"Did you enjoy that?"

Dominique hesitated before he said, "I liked being with my mother. But a boy's place is among boys. It wasn't good that my head was filled with the women's stories. So I got used to the lessons. I had to." He lifted his shoulders in a small shrug.

"I see."

"I wish I could go back." Whatever teasing he'd

ever put up with, even the smacks on the head, were better than this.

"But you can't go back if you have been cast out."

He didn't trust himself to speak. He didn't want to start crying again.

"The Estorians send their boys away for being silent. Interesting."

The events of the previous night pressed into his consciousness, dark and overwhelming. Had he really been banished? How could his people have done this to him?

"So, at the story ceremony, nothing came to you at all?"

Dominique's shame made him drop his gaze to the floor. He studied the small, even ridges in the dirt. She must have raked it while he was sleeping.

"Only the women's stories came to me," he admitted miserably. "The stories of Tara. And like I said, the women's stories are no good. Not for a boy."

"Hmm."

"I have a year and a day to learn to hear the Stories from the Grand Tellers Beyond. Only then can I go back."

"Where do you think you might find these 'Stories from Beyond'?"

"I don't know if there is a place, a particular place," Dominique admitted. "The tellers, the proper tellers, are supposed to be able to hear Stories anywhere. The Stories come from beyond the edge of the sky, but nobody ever goes there."

"So how do your people hear these Stories?"

"It's the men who hear the Stories of Truth. The women teach their stories to the girls. That's why it's easier to be a girl."

"Do you really think so?"

Dominique looked away. Maybe he had offended his host.

"I mean, they don't have to do anything special—like listen for the *Truth*."

"Don't men share their stories with each other?"

"Yes. Well, they tell the Stories they hear from beyond to the rest of the clan. You can tell your own Stories and the historical stories over and over but no man is allowed to tell another man's Story. That would be . . . stealing. You can get banished for that, too—at any age."

Bethusela nodded. "How many stories does each man know?"

"That depends. Some know only a few. But the best tellers know hundreds and hundreds and each Story they tell fits exactly with what the listeners need to hear."

"Like Tobias Rondolo?"

"You've heard of Tobias?" Dominique stared quizzically at Bethusela.

She nodded. "At the court of Lord Andaglio. I was delivering special mushrooms to the royal physician. I heard Tobias Rondolo tell a story of a warrior lord who planned an invasion of Lord Andaglio's lands."

"Tobias is one of the best."

"It was a clever story, yes. Tobias Rondolo

spoke of Lord Andaglio's victory in great, gory detail . . . even though the battle hadn't happened yet. Rondolo was well paid for his tale, as I recall."

"The best tellers are wealthy men," Dominique agreed.

Bethusela nodded and sipped her tea. "The Estorians I've met at markets or festivals, they've always held a good crowd. But I suppose a silent Estorian wouldn't be much good as a wage earner."

"I don't . . . I think . . . I . . ." Dominique stammered, suddenly feeling very sorry for himself. A silent Estorian wasn't good for anything.

"Drink your tea."

Dominique gazed longingly at the closed door of the cottage. What would his mother be doing now?

"You can't go back because your people won't be there. Your people are travellers, am I right?"

Dominique nodded. Of course his people would have moved on. The various clans would already have headed off in different directions. They wouldn't come together again until the following year.

Dominique drew a hiccuping breath and tried to disguise it by taking a quick drink of his strong tea. He'd never tasted anything like it. Without the honey, it probably would have been quite bitter. The warm liquid loosened his tongue.

"I don't know how I'm supposed to know when I hear the Truth," he said when Bethusela stood and reached up to a high shelf. Her fingers closed on a blue jar tucked behind several clumps of moss. She unscrewed the top and Dominique's nostrils flared as a strong aroma filled the small room.

"Eucalyptus balm," she said, taking some on her fingertips. "Very soothing after a long day outside." Bethusela rubbed the greasy substance onto her head, her fingers moving in slow, thoughtful circles over her smooth dome. "And good for those welts, too.

"Truth," she continued, as she smeared the pungent salve over Dominique's mottled skin. "Can you ever rely on a truth that comes from somewhere outside you?"

"Yes, when it comes from the Place Beyond. . . ." he faltered.

"And how, my boy, if you don't know exactly how to find the place beyond the edge of the sky, how can you know for certain that's where the stories come from?"

Dominique opened his mouth and then closed it again without saying anything. It was all so confusing.

"You may not know exactly when or how you'll hear your first story, and you obviously don't know what that story will be." She set the jar back on the shelf before she continued. "But you do know where you are going, right?"

Dominique closed his eyes and shook his head. "I think I'm supposed to go to the Cave of Departure. But I don't understand why, or what I'll find there."

Bethusela took his mug and tipped the dregs into the fire. The liquid hit the logs with a hiss and sizzled away into ever-smaller bubbles. She poured fresh peppermint tea from a second, smaller teapot into the heavy stone mugs.

"Drink this."

Dominique sipped at the delicious hot liquid and listened. Bethusela kneeled beside him so their heads were now at the same level.

"I can tell you the way to the cave, though I can't take you there. I'm getting too old and the journey is too difficult. The Cave of Departure is a place where journeys of all kinds begin. The Estorians are not the only ones who have used the place over the centuries. But your journey should not end there. The contrary is true."

Bethusela looked up from her tea and nodded twice, quickly, as if she had made up her mind about something. She eased herself off her knees, opened a small wooden cupboard door set into the wall, and pulled out a sack.

"Take this."

Dominique took the empty bag. It was soft, made of deerskin, with a drawstring at the top.

"You will find what you need for your journey at the cave. For hundreds of years questers have stopped there to gather supplies. There is an understanding that at the end of your journey you will return to the cave, replace what you have used, and add something of your own besides."

"Thank you."

"All journeys really begin when they end. You'll see when you get—"

Bethusela stopped mid-sentence and went to the door. She stood with her hand resting on the carved doorknob. Dominique had heard nothing but Bethusela listened intently. When she pulled the door open, Dominique was surprised to see darkness beyond. How long *had* he slept?

Navina, who had been dozing on one foot on Dominique's shoulder, awoke with a peep and leaped into the air. She flew twice around the small room before coming to rest on the mantelpiece on top of a long, curved horn, which looked like it had come from some animal at least twice the size of a good-sized bull. Navina hopped along to the pointed end and glared at the black space of the doorway.

14

PARTING

The women sang as they plucked the fat pheasants, carefully saving the long golden tail feathers for the Protector's harvest headdress.

"Well, are you coming in or not?" Bethusela asked.

The fox darted inside, as quick and lively as earlier he had been sleepy and content. Dominique could hardly see the animal's face for Vulpescio held a plump ruffed grouse in his jaws.

"Oh, delicious, Vulpescio. I'll make a nice stew, shall I?" The fox didn't answer but dropped the bird at Bethusela's feet, turned, and slipped back out into the night. Up on the mantelpiece, Navina skittered from end to end of the horn, making it rock back and forth with each pass.

"Calm down, Navina," Dominique said, moving to stand beside the fire. He held out his finger but the little bird refused to budge. She did deign to lower her head so he could scratch her favourite spot. With his little finger Dominique touched the feathers on the back of her head and neck, lifting them and then letting them fall back into place.

"I'll clean the grouse shortly," Bethusela said with a satisfied grin. "Vulpescio and I, we look after each other, we do. Now, where were we?"

Bethusela eased herself onto a wooden bench made from a rough-hewn plank fastened to two stumps. "Come, sit up here beside me. Bring your tea."

Dominique squeezed onto the bench beside the old woman. He couldn't help staring at the dead bird lying in front of them.

"I was about to ask you if you could do a different job—just in case you don't find your stories."

"No. There is no other job for an Estorian man." He shook his head firmly. That, at least, was one thing he knew for certain. "Anyone who can't do his job gets banished. Or . . ." *Executed.*

"Or?"

"Or . . . punished severely."

Being in Bethusela's warm house made his head feel thick and stupid with a strange longing to sleep again. Dominique stroked the smooth deerskin sack in his lap and wondered what he would find at the cave to fill it. His thoughts drifted woozily to some place in his future he couldn't clearly imagine.

A log popped in the fire and Dominique jumped. He wanted to talk, to ask more questions, but once again the silence that had plagued him his whole life held his tongue immobile and useless.

Bethusela gathered up the grouse, held the bird by its scaly feet and unceremoniously chopped off its head.

Dominique shrank back. Navina squawked as loudly as a hawk.

"You're not used to watching women work?"

Dominique's eyes widened and he shook his head. Not any more. Not for a long, long time. His mother had made such a point of raising him prop-erly after the big fight with Panna that day on the riverbank. Ever since, she had kept him well away from the women's chores, as was proper for an Estorian boy. He could hardly remember ever being allowed to watch the fire-starting rituals or the slaughter and dressing of food once living.

Bethusela held the severed neck over a bowl until the bird had stopped bleeding. Then, still holding the plump grouse by its feet, she dipped it into a large cauldron of boiling water. Steam rose from the water but Bethusela didn't seem to feel the heat. Rocking back on her heels, she drew the bird from the pot, let it drip a few moments, and blotted it with a thick cloth. This she placed on her lap. Bethusela lay the steaming bird on top of the cloth and began to pluck the feathers.

This was too much for Navina. Dominique scrambled to his feet and darted over to his bird, who seemed paralyzed with horror, and gently picked her up. Her tiny heart hammered wildly beneath his fingers and he slipped her back into his pocket so she wouldn't have to see any more.

Dominique closed his eyes. He felt quite ill. This crazy old woman was wrong to prepare the grouse in front of him.

"Not a bad idea," Bethusela said, "closing your eyes. Why don't you lie back down while I finish this. I'll let you know when the dawn comes calling for you."

Dominique nodded and sank back into the furs. It made no sense that he was so incredibly weary so soon after awakening.

"And, Dominique? I'm sorry I frightened your bird."

Dominique awoke again when Bethusela's crooked old fingers brushed gently across his forehead. The cottage smelled of a rich, hearty stew, and immediately Dominique's mouth began to water.

Bethusela pressed a heel of bread into his hand.

"Eat this," she said, as she handed Dominique the deerskin sack, no longer empty. "I've prepared a bundle for you with a few things you will need. "There's a small pot of stew and some more bread in the bag for later."

Bethusela poked a finger at his chest. "You can wear that, if you like. It's a bit big, but at least you won't look like a spotted fleacat." Dominique looked down. Sometime while he had been sleeping, Bethusela had dressed him in an old cotton shift. The undergarment was baggy, but at least it was soft against his skin.

"Thank you."

Dominique ate quickly. He followed the bread

with a large mug of peppermint tea. As he ate, Bethusela gave him instructions.

"Travel due east until the sun is directly overhead."

East. Just the sound of the word filled him with dread, but Dominique nodded for her to go on.

"You will come to a river, the River Epilobium. Beware of Lagrace, the river serpent. Gaze not upon the serpent's face, upon either of her faces. . . ."

Dominique shuddered. Bethusela didn't need to tell him why. Everyone knew the stories well. The two-headed serpent lured children into her watery lair by singing magical songs.

" . . . because you know what happens if you look into Lagrace's ugly eyes."

Dominique made a choking sound.

"Exactly." She poked at the fire. "If you do take so much as a peek, heaviness will seep into your limbs. Like a stone you will sink to the bottom of the river, and there, Lagrace will devour you."

Dominique clutched the deerskin bag to his chest.

"The Cave of Departure is on the far side of the River Epilobium."

"Is there a bridge?"

Bethusela shook her head. "Lagrace would never allow such a thing."

"Then how do I get across?"

"Swim, of course. You can swim, can't you?"

Dominique nodded, though he wondered how fast he would have to move to outdistance the river serpent.

"Swim quickly and you will soon reach the other side of the river. From there you will be able to see the tusk of Rain Mountain. From the far side of the river it's about two days' walk to the base of the tusk. Once you arrive, listen for the sound of falling water. Follow the water and you will come to the Dancing Falls. Behind the falling curtain is your cave."

Dominique clenched his fists. As the old woman continued, adding details of landmarks to watch for and reminding him to stay clear of roughweed, Dominique felt anger rising within him. The rage bit at the back of his throat and he felt as if a wave of liquid fire might spew forth from some deep place inside him, searing everything in its path. It wasn't Bethusela who fed his fury, he realized. It was Bertolescu. Why had the Protector bothered with the sham of this journey? He should have killed Dominique right away and saved him the agony of a terrifying death in the muddy bottom of a river or in the jaws of a crazed yagabono.

"Be careful, though. Once you are on the far side of the river you will be in the land of the incubus."

"Incubus?"

"Dark creatures of the air. They prefer to travel at night and avoid places underground or where they don't have room to fly freely. Before night falls, find a resting place below ground level. Dig a trench to sleep in, or find shelter inside. There used to be a few shepherd's shacks along the way. Look to see if any are left." She paused and squeezed her eyes closed. "It is not an easy thing you must do." She coughed, a dry, nervous hack, and then fixed her gaze somewhere between Dominique's chin and his chest. "Now. Go. You have a long way to travel."

At the thought of actually leaving the snug cottage, Dominique's rage dissipated and in its place he felt the icy trickle of terror spilling through his veins.

"Could I stay here? Please?"

Bethusela shook her head sadly. "It would never do. You are not a forest dweller. It would be wrong for me to let you stop here."

The door pushed open before Dominique could ask who would even notice if he stayed. Vulpescio slipped in and hopped onto the pile of furs. He turned three times in place, tucked his nose under his great plume of a tail, closed his eyes, and instantly fell asleep.

"The day has begun," Bethusela said.

"And I must go," Dominique said, reluctantly slinging the sack over his shoulder and stepping outside. "Thank you," he said.

Bethusela raised one hand in a small, stiff wave. Then Dominique squared his shoulders and turned to face the direction of the rising sun.

THE RIVER EPILOBIUM

The winged dragon shrieked at the boy, lashing
its tail from side to side. Flames licked at
Rimbel's tunic but the boy stood his ground.

"It can't be much farther, can it?"

Navina swooped ahead along the path through
the trees and landed lightly on a supple branch. She
twittered as the twig swayed up and down.

"Don't get too far ahead! You don't want to get
lost, do you?"

Navina fluttered back onto Dominique's
shoulder and perched for a while as he walked
steadily eastward. The sun crept higher. Dominique
knew that each step brought the river closer and,
with each step, his breathing quickened. The forest
was less dense now as they neared the plains.

Dominique let his fingertips brush against the
trunks of the last trees, caressing them as he passed.

And then he was at the edge of the forest, grinding his teeth. He paused, surveying the wide expanse of rolling grasslands ahead of him before doggedly continuing on. Less than half an hour later, the River Epilobium wound into view and sweat started to trickle down his sides.

Navina didn't seem to share his worries. Out in the open grasslands she swooped low over the grasses, stopping frequently to sample the fresh, green shoots. She darted from a clump of rich tipple grass to a bank of sweet, wild spangle. She nipped off only the succulent tips before fluttering across the path to hang upside down from a fat seed head of a giant stand of phlimmox grass, which was already taller than Dominique.

When she spotted a clump of squat dragonberry bushes, she let out a chitter-peep and flew into the heart of the prickly branches. No matter how Dominique pleaded, she refused to relinquish her grip on the branches until the feathers of her red breast were smeared with deep maroon dribbles of dragonberry juice.

"Come on. You've had enough. We don't want to cross that river at night."

The bird finally allowed him to pick her up and they continued on, Navina now contentedly preening herself on top of Dominique's head. Dominique wished he could look anywhere else than at the mesmerizing river. He watched with dread as the shimmering ribbon drew closer, a blue-green snake curling its way across the plains between him and the distant mountains. Lit by the hot spring sun, the lush greenery looked inviting, the kind of place a travelling clan might stop to have lunch, the kind of place where a father and son might rest a while together. The thought shook him and he stopped.

Had his father ever been here? Had Boris Elnedo ever stood still and listened to this wind? Heard the honking calls of the Kremland snow geese as they flew overhead? Another sound soon drifted to Dominique's ears: the voice of the river, gurgling and swishing its way across the plains.

"Papa . . ."

An echo of his father's voice answered, *Nothing? You have heard nothing?* But it wasn't the words themselves that struck Dominique now. It was the memory of his father's hesitation as he spoke them. Boris Elnedo's forehead had creased with worry but then he had turned away. The one thing his father had never expressed was surprise. It was almost as if he had always known Dominique would never hear a Story from Beyond. So why hadn't he said anything? Tried to help?

Dominique cleared his throat. To help, his father would have had to stay with his family—at least sometimes. Maybe his father had wanted Dominique to fail. Tears pricked at Dominique's eyes and he quickly bent down to pick up a stone. He hurled it as far as he could, blinking back the tears even as he cried out, "Pa-paaaaaa!"

Startled, two tempala bucks bounded across the spare and beautiful grasslands spread before him. Dominique watched them until they disappeared in the distance. His gaze followed the river's course south until it disappeared into a grey haze at the horizon. Carnillo, the largest seaport on the island of Tanga, lay to the south, but from where he stood he could see no sign of the city. Tanga was huge, by far the largest island in the Drasil Archipelago. Dominique knew he could travel for days without coming across anyone else, especially not here in the east.

The distant Misty Mountains were clearer now. A jagged line of ochre-coloured stone topped with snow, the mountains pushed up against a vast blue sky. Though the plains east of the river were prime grazing territory, Dominique couldn't see a single sheep, never mind any shepherd shacks. A cloud passed in front of the sun and Dominique shuddered.

"We can't stand here all day," he said aloud, trying to give himself courage to continue.

Navina puffed herself up and then tugged on his ear. He reached up and rubbed his finger over the top of her beak. She leaned into the caress and closed her eyes.

The land at Dominique's feet sloped towards the distant river. A flock of yellow tittle swishes rose and turned as one, a cloud of birds fluttering in a wide arc before settling into a new patch of grass. The landscape was so beautiful he couldn't believe it was really home to such creatures. "It can't be *that* bad, can it?" he asked Navina. "The Protector wouldn't have sent us here if it couldn't be done, would he?" Navina cocked her head to one side and clicked her beak. Or would he? Maybe he knew exactly what lay ahead. "Well, Bethusela wouldn't have let us leave if she thought we were going to die."

Dominique lifted his sack to his shoulder and set off again, too nervous to think about feeding his grumbling stomach. Now that he was out in the open and away from the Aspen Woods, the lightly trodden path through the grass peeled backwards beneath his feet at an alarming rate.

The low swish and gurgle of the River Epilobium grew louder. Soon, he could hear something else, too. He stopped again and listened, his sack sliding slowly to the ground.

"Shh, Navina." The bird stopped her twittering and tipped her head forward. Her red crest stood up with curiosity.

The sound was unlike any he had ever heard before—a delicate whistle, clear and sweet, a wavering musical call. The melody was elusive, almost not a song at all. Surely that couldn't be Lagrace?

Dominique moved closer until he was at the top of the riverbank. He sat on his bottom and slid down through the mud and grasses. The musical whistle was so lovely it filtered into his thoughts, lulling him with its easy beauty. There was nothing bad about this music—it was just the song of the river, that was all.

Everything was suddenly clear now. His people thought nothing of rejecting boys they didn't like. It would be nothing for them to tell lies about serpents to stop children playing too close to the water. Dominique kneeled, suddenly thirsty, and dipped his cupped hands into the water. He drank deeply, the cold, delicious water dribbling through his fingers, splashing down his chin. He closed his eyes and plunged his whole head into the river. Then he shook himself so a spray of water drops showered the air around him. Navina hopped in and out of the shallow water at the river's edge, drinking tiny sips and fluttering her wings with excitement.

The mellifluous whistling melody filled the air, seeping into every corner of Dominique's mind, filling it so there was no space to think about where he was supposed to be going.

Dominique looked up and down along the riverbank, half expecting to see a musician with a flute, or perhaps a shepherd with his pipe, but he was completely alone. The surface of the River Epilobium rippled gently in the sunshine as it drifted past.

On the far side of the river the graceful finger-tips of weeping willow branches trailed in the water. "I'll meet you over there," he said to Navina, shooing her off. She took another sip of water, shook herself, and then flapped into the air. She circled once overhead then swooped away over the water, an iridescent flash against the deep blue of the river.

When she had disappeared into the trees on the far bank, Dominique leaned forward again for another drink. The musical whistling grew louder as his head came closer to the water. Intrigued, he turned his head to the side and put his ear to the rippled surface. The sounds changed, so now the music was slightly muffled and distorted, but it was quite clearly coming from under the water.

Dominique glanced up at the sun, now high in the sky. This was as good a time as any to begin the crossing. He stripped off the old shift Bethusela had given him and stuffed it into the deerskin sack. There was no sign of the serpent—perhaps she was hunting elsewhere. He knotted the cord of the sack tightly and then tied it around his waist before stepping into the swirling waters of the river. With such glorious music to listen to, it was no wonder the serpent made her home here in the river.

The current tugged playfully at his ankles and Dominique waded out into deeper water. He pushed aside the reeds growing close to shore and kept going. With each step, the fluid music swelled rich and lovely.

When he stood waist deep, he took a deep breath and sank to his knees, allowing the murky water to slip over him. Ignoring the cold, he crouched lower until he was completely submerged. His ears, his head, filled with the peculiar, melancholy whistling until it felt like the music was coming from inside him, had become a part of him.

When he could hold his breath no longer, he stood, bursting through the surface of the water, coughing and sputtering and shaking his head clear.

In the next moment he heard two things—a frantic yipping and yowling from the riverbank behind him, and a slow, swooshing roar from under the water in the deeper part of the river before him.

He turned to see what was making the racket behind him.

"Vulpescio!" he shouted.

Bethusela's fox raced back and forth along the riverbank, yelping and whimpering.

Dominique froze. Under the water strange currents tugged and pulled at his legs.

Lagrace! Something brushed against Dominique's bare legs and he screamed.

Vulpescio froze, then dropped flat on his belly. At first, Dominique couldn't see what the fox was doing. The music filled the air around him, insistent, sad with longing. Dominique fought the urge to turn around to see where the sound was coming from. He concentrated on Bethusela's words, repeating them over and over again in his mind.

Gaze not upon the serpent's face, upon either of her faces. . . .

At the water's edge Vulpescio pressed his chin into the soft mud and covered his eyes with his paws. He repeated the motion until Dominique shouted, "Yes!" and closed his own eyes. Squeezing them tightly shut he turned around carefully until he thought he must be facing the opposite bank. Then he sank slowly into the water and struck out, splashing awkwardly.

As his ears filled, the music grew louder and louder. At first, the melody was sweet and playful. Dominique fought the rising temptation to open his eyes and peek.

He stroked desperately, blindly, and dragged himself through the churning water. The tone of the whistling changed—now it was ominous, threatening.

Beneath him, the water rolled and tossed and he

130

threw his arms out to the side to keep from being sucked under. Whirlpools twisted him this way and that, and then something scaly dragged across his foot.

Dominique's mouth filled with water when he screamed. He paddled in place, coughing and spitting out gritty mouthfuls of water. *Keep going,* he told himself. Dominique rolled onto his back, kicking out with his feet, the water heaving all around him.

Another stroke. Another stroke.

But his arms, exhausted, refused to respond. They trailed beside him, weak and useless, too tired to stop him from drifting downstream heading out to sea. For all he knew, he could be floating around and around in circles.

Keep your eyes shut. Gaze not upon her faces.

Where was the current? The water churned, pulling Dominique in a tight spiral.

Swim!

He twisted back onto his stomach and tried to claw his way through the water, kicking weakly now, bashing his heavy arms through the foaming waves.

"Go away!"

Lagrace paid no attention. Somewhere beneath him, the serpent stirred the water.

Where was the far shore?

Gaze not upon either of her faces.

Dominique had to rest. He stopped kicking, rolled over on his back again, and stretched his arms out sideways. He drifted, turning this way and that as the water beneath him swirled and gurgled.

The strange music sang, taunting him, tempting him to relax and open his eyes. As he lay there, floating in the swirl of music and terror, Dominique felt the water by his head heave as some massive weight broke the surface. Drips fell on his face as that same something rose above him, something with a cool, sweet breath, a creature singing the watery music of death.

"Agggh!" Dominique screamed at the top of his lungs and then disappeared under the surface. In total panic he opened his eyes and right before him saw the glittering scales of the serpent's sinewy side slipping and turning through the water.

He clenched his eyes shut again and kicked hard for the surface. Coughing and sputtering he struggled for air and then hoarsely screamed again and again.

To his surprise, he noticed that when he was screaming he could not hear the music.

"Go away!" he shouted and started swimming blindly once again.

"Go away, leave me alone, I'm swimming, I'm going to the far side of the river, I'm swimming. . . ."

As long as he was making a sound, he could not hear the music. His limbs responded, pushing him through the water.

"I'mmmmm swimmmming. . . ." When he drew out the *mmm* sounds, even this humming was enough to keep the enchanting music at bay. He swam with his face in the water and hummed at the same time.

Beneath him, the creature grew bolder and Dominique scrunched his eyes more tightly shut. Lagrace pushed at his sides and grabbed at his feet. He swam on, dragging in great choking breaths, frantic to reach his destination before his ebbing strength failed him completely.

When he rolled on his back and propelled himself along with kicks, he sang and talked to himself, blocking out the song of Lagrace. Twice the cool slither of the creature's tongue licked at his bare ankles. He kicked out as hard as he could and sang louder, feeling the pull of the river and then swimming across the current.

"Aggggh!"

Sticky tendrils dragged across his face and Dominique lashed out wildly. The more he struck out, the more the strings caught at his arms and whipped at his face.

"Put your feet down!"

At first, Dominique thought it was a trick. The strings slipping over his face were Lagrace's nets and the voice another way the serpent lured her prey. Dominique had come this far—he wasn't going to be fooled so easily.

"Boy in the river!" the voice shouted again. "Put your feet down! You should be able to reach the bottom. Try to stand up."

16

THE GOOD KNIGHT

*The travellers parted at the southeast gate of the
city wall. If each had only kept his promise,
both would still be alive today.*

With his eyes still clamped shut, Dominique dropped
his legs down, ready to kick out again if anything
grabbed him to suck him under. But nothing clamped
around his legs. Instead, he felt the soft mud of the
river bottom oozing between his toes. He swatted at
the thin, sinewy ropes swinging into his face.

"This way! Come towards my voice!" The man
sounded very close and not in the least watery or
musical. "Never mind the willow branches—push
them aside. That's it!"

Dominique swatted at the hanging branches and
made his way towards the voice calling words of
encouragement. The river water became shallower
with each unsteady step he took.

Behind him, Dominique heard a furious thrashing and churning and the water around him bubbled and boiled.

"Don't look back! That's a boy—keep coming!"

Water splashed and sprayed over his back and Dominique whimpered.

"That's it. A few more steps . . ."

A pair of strong hands grabbed Dominique's arms and pulled him to safety.

Dominique felt himself being half dragged, half carried up the riverbank. He sank into the grass and began to sob.

"Why the tears now, boy? Lagrace, the old water bag, she should be the one weeping and wailing! You've cheated her out of a good meal, you have."

Through his tears, Dominique felt himself smiling. It was a strange thing to find funny, the fact he had made a mortal enemy of the river serpent.

"You can open your eyes, you can. She won't come out of the water to get you."

Dominique swiped at his eyes with the back of his hand, cursing the hot tears seeping out. He didn't dare open them. Somewhere high above, Navina chirruped and chattered.

"Come on then, lad. You can't get far by walking around with your eyes shut. You'll bash your nose on a tree trunk, or fall back into the river, or tumble into a yagabono pit."

Yagabonos. Dominique shivered. He may have escaped Lagrace's snapping jaws, but it gave him little confidence he'd be able to avoid the peculiar marsupials of the high plains.

"They're easy enough to spot," the voice went on. "The mounds of excavated dirt give the yagabono pits away. But you'll smell the sons of pit-dwellers long before you see them. Disgusting stench, it is. The abandoned pits, though, once they've had a chance to air out—they make excellent temporary shelters when you're hiding from an incubus. You know about getting underground at night, don't you?"

Dominique nodded and groaned softly but still didn't open his eyes. He wished somehow he could wake up and find himself back in his bed in the family hut. The flesh on his arms was pimpled with cold and his stomach growled.

"Just look at you! For someone who has just been swimming, you are filthy!"

At that, Dominique looked down at himself. He was covered in greenish-brown mud. Reeds hung from the deerskin bag still fastened to his waist by the tough cord.

He glanced behind him. The river was mostly hidden by the row of graceful weeping willows. The river's edge seemed so peaceful. The breeze swept the faintest whisper of music towards him and Dominique quickly closed his eyes again.

"Not to worry. You're quite safe now—from that old snake, anyway. She never leaves the water. Hungry?"

Dominique opened his eyes and this time found himself staring at a short, round man with an enormous belly.

"Sir Riley at your service."

The man bowed deeply and swept his sword in a broad arc through the air in front of him before sliding it smoothly into an ornate leather scabbard.

"Glad I didn't have to use this after all. Even if I'd managed to get her in the soft spot in her belly, it would only have brought more trouble."

"To kill without cause is a sign of weakness," Dominique said, finding his tongue in time to repeat a lesson that had been drilled into his head when he was younger.

"Not at all!" Sir Riley said. "Do you know nothing about river serpents? I'd kill six before breakfast, if it made sense."

Embarrassed, Dominique looked down at his filthy bare feet and shivered again. A breeze had come up in the shade of the willows and he hopped from foot to foot to try to warm up.

"Rip open the belly of a creature like Lagrace and what do you think comes out?"

Dominique shook his head. He had no idea. "Blood?"

"Phaw! Nonsense. A hundred baby serpents is what. Many would say the sacrifice of one boy is better than freeing one hundred little monsters from their mother's belly. What do you think?"

"I . . . I . . . th-think I should t-t-take off these underleggings," Dominique said through chattering teeth. Navina swooped around him in a graceful arc and then soared back up into a pebblenut tree. Now that Dominique was safe on dry land, Navina seemed quite content to snap open the tiny nuts that hung in clusters from the tree's reddish-brown branches. The tough shells sprinkled down as she feasted on the tender nutmeat inside.

"Why, yes. Of course—what am I thinking, giving you a lecture on the ethics of serpent slaughter while you're freezing to death?"

Sir Riley rummaged about in a pile of things on the ground nearby. He moved aside a suit of armour, a sword, and a shield and then lifted up a sack similar to Dominique's. From this bag Sir Riley drew first a flint and stone and then a package wrapped in fabric coated with some kind of oil or resin. Inside was a bundle of small twigs. Using the dry kindling, he soon had a crackling fire blazing at the edge of the trees.

Dominique peeled off his wet underleggings and spread them on the ground by the fire. Still shivering, he fiddled with the soggy knots in the cord of his sack. When he had managed to get it open, he pulled out his soaking wet shirt and ceremonial feather tunic. He tipped the rest of the sack's contents out on the ground. Bethusela had added several things to the bag including a paring knife, some fishing line, and a small woollen blanket. These, too, he spread out to dry.

"Hmmmm, appetizing," Sir Riley remarked as Dominique wrung out a soggy lump that had once been half a loaf of bread.

A small pot, wrapped tightly in the same kind of waterproof oilcloth as Sir Riley's fire-starting twigs, had fared better. When Dominique unwrapped it and pried off the lid, his eyes widened with delight.

"Stew!" he said, starting to feel better as the fire warmed him.

"Excellent!"

"Would you like some?" Dominique asked, remembering his manners.

"Why, thank you. We could have it with some of my bread," Sir Riley said.

Dominique nodded and nestled the pot into the edge of the fire.

"Put the lid back on or you'll be eating more ash than anything else."

Dominique did as he was told. He wondered why the portly little man knew the women's secrets of fire-making and cooking. He thought it might be rude to ask outright if the man did not have a wife or at least a cicefyrian-wench to perform such duties.

"Who are you?" Dominique asked finally, giving in to his curiosity with what he hoped was not too forward an inquiry.

"You are a fine one to ask! It's not that unusual to see a knight like me patrolling the far reaches of the kingdom. It's far more unusual to see a boy such as yourself swimming across the River Epilobium, eyes shut, covered in mud and slime and singing away as loud as can be. I might ask, with good reason, who are *you?*"

"Dominique, sir." The boy was stunned that this roly-poly fellow was a knight. That explained the armour, but where was his horse? "Dominique Elnedo."

"Ahhh, a Campriano. One of Lord Emberto's men?"

Dominique shook his head. How strange. That was the second time he had been mistaken for one of the liars. *Not an honest Storyteller among the lot*, Uncle Sebastien had once said. *They make Stories up!* Marcus had told him. *The good ones see the truth and they leave*, his mother had answered when he asked if every Campriano was bad, a liar.

"No!" he said hotly. "I am an Estorian. Son of Dania and Boris Elnedo."

"Ah-ha . . ." the knight said, though he sounded unconvinced.

"Why would I lie?" Dominique challenged.

"Why not? What storyteller has ever spoken the truth?"

"We do! We Estorians always do."

Sir Riley fed a few more sticks into the fire and lifted the lid of the stew pot. "Almost ready," he said, giving it a stir. "Very well, young Estorian. Perhaps you would be so kind as to tell me a story. An honest story."

Dominique bit the inside of his cheek. What he would give to be able to open his mouth and spin the kind of yarn the knight expected! But, of course, nothing came to him. He hung his head.

"I can't."

"What do you mean, you can't?"

"That's the problem. That's why I was banished. No Stories have ever come to me. I was sent away to find them. Stories, I mean. Or, to learn how to hear them."

"Hmmm." Sir Riley poked at the bubbling pot with a thick stick and pushed the stew out of the flames. "Eat," he said. "I'm hungry."

Dominique heaved a huge sigh of relief. Maybe filling his belly would provide comfort enough for the knight, and Dominique wouldn't have to embarrass himself with the blushing and stammering that would surely result if he tried to tell a Story.

17

BUILDING FIRES

"You must be brave, you must be strong, you must be foolish," said the witch, and she sent Ambroglio on his way.

The two travellers said nothing as they tucked into Bethusela's hearty stew. Rich, meaty juices dribbled down Dominique's chin as he gobbled his way through the meal. With every mouthful, Dominique felt braver. Escaping the watery grave hadn't been so difficult. Sir Riley mopped up the last of the gravy with his bread and then leaned back in the grass, his stubby fingers drumming idly on his bulging tummy. He studied the boy with his watery blue eyes until Dominique squirmed under the man's gaze.

"As a knight of the House of Ronwyn, it is my sworn duty to help those in need," the knight said finally. "But I have no knowledge of the way

Estorians come to storytelling, and so, I fear, I can offer you no guidance."

Dominique hadn't expected any. He was happy enough that Sir Riley had appeared on the riverbank when he had and that he happened to have dry kindling in his sack.

"The House of Ronwyn? Is that far from here?"

"Aye. North of Lake Epilobium. Lord Ronwyn's lands have been quiet of late, but he's worried about the troubles with Lord Emberto. The most powerful man in Carnillo is not a fellow to be ignored. Lord Ronwyn's army is strong but only as effective as the news he receives."

Riley worked a sharp stick between his teeth to free a bit of gristle.

Dominique hoped the rest of Ronwyn's men were in better shape than Riley.

"So, you don't think I'd be much of a soldier?" Riley asked, following Dominique's gaze and moving his other hand in a slow circle over his rotund stomach. "Hah! Don't be embarrassed. I know I'm a little plump."

A little plump? Dominique couldn't imagine how Riley managed to climb aboard his warhorse.

"Do all knights have to fight?"

"Do fish have fins?" Riley grunted and winked. "Even the best of us have to yield to old age eventually. I have been a knight for many, many years. When I was a younger, fitter man I fought alongside Ronwyn's father in the Battle of Chanmari."

Even in top fighting form, Riley seemed far too short to be a soldier. He wasn't much taller than

Dominique.

"Knights never retire, you know. We find other ways to be useful. I'm a scout now. A wanderer. Occasionally I have to rescue someone. Most of the time I try to stay out of trouble's way. I watch. I report back to Lord Ronwyn."

"Where is your horse?"

"Horse? Great bellies on legs, they are! I have a donkey called Pliny. A modest appetite and a grand sense of humour!" The knight giggled.

"Where is he?"

"Pliny? Grazing. He'll come when I call. Now, tell me—where are you going?"

"East," Dominique said, looking across the expanse of grassland between where they sat close to the willows and the distant mountains. Only the occasional spindly tree broke the landscape. He could just make out the tusk of Rain Mountain in the distance and his heart gave a little jump. How far was it now? Two days' walk? Maybe three? Maybe he shouldn't have been so quick to share his meagre food supplies.

"Why would a boy like you want to go to the mountains?" Riley wasn't laughing any more. "Fools perish where mortals shouldn't tread."

Dominique hesitated before continuing. "I have to go to Rain Mountain. To the tusk. I can do it. I got across the river."

"No need to get defensive, my boy. There's nothing up there except the Cave of Departure."

Dominique leaned forward.

Riley's eyes squinted as he looked towards the

craggy peaks of the Misty Mountains. "Well, I'll be. You're the second fool today who is heading in that direction."

"What!?" Dominique's heart flip-flopped. Maybe someone from his clan was coming to help? Maybe someone had overtaken him while he was resting at Bethusela's. "Who was it? Did you talk to . . . ?"

"Too far away to talk to. It was someone on horseback, wearing a black cloak bearing a red eagle."

"A Campriano?"

"I don't know anyone else who would wear the blood eagle symbol."

Dominique sank back in disappointment. A Campriano was the last sort of person he'd want to run into on a journey like this.

"So you don't know where he was going?"

"To be honest, there's not much else to see in these parts, other than the cave. Though he might have been a bounty hunter looking for leranons. They're fetching top prices in mainland markets these days. But, no, I didn't get close enough to chat. The rider seemed in a hurry. He was pushing his horses fast."

"Horses? He had more than one?"

"A riding horse and a pack horse. He must have come a fair distance. At least from Carnillo, I'd say."

Dominique slumped back against a tree trunk.

"Don't look so glum. Chances are he will have come and gone by the time you get there. Even if he's also headed for the cave, you are on foot."

"Have you ever seen it? The cave?"

"Ah, yes. I've been there several times, though more often when I was younger. At the end of my last quest I left a lovely dagger—sharp as anything. You should look for it—if you make it to the cave alive. It might still be there and it would be handy. You'll recognize it by the donkey's head carved on the wooden handle. You have no weapons, do you?"

"Only Bethusela's knife."

Sir Riley picked it up. "This? Wouldn't kill a mouse."

That might have been true, but the knife was more than Dominique had owned when he had left the clan.

"You should waste no more time getting to the cave so you can find some proper equipment. I have nothing to spare, I'm afraid. I travel with only the bare necessities." The knight looked for the sun, already lower than the tops of the willows. "I don't mean to state the obvious, but you have no time to waste idling about here. Have you any more food?"

Bethusela's sack had also contained a pouch of uncooked rice as well as some dried kidney beans. These had swollen into a thick, soggy mess during the river crossing.

"Don't throw that out," Riley said. "Here." He rooted around in his own bag and pulled out a small pouch full of ground spices. He peeled back the edge of Dominique's package of rice and beans and sprinkled some herbs over the top. He stirred them with a pudgy fingertip.

"Wrap that up again and when you're ready to

eat, just add some to a pot of boiling water. Your stew pot will work. It won't look like much, but at least your belly will be full. You have a flint, do you?"

Dominique shrugged. "Bethusela—a . . . a friend of mine packed the sack."

He turned the deerskin sack inside out and discovered several pockets sewn inside. In one was a candle, in another a flint and a small piece of steel. By the time he had explored all the pockets he had quite a pile of useful items, including a length of strong cord, three fish hooks, and a heavy sewing needle.

"Your friend Bethusela knows the needs of a traveller. How are your fire-making skills?"

"I'm not . . . I don't . . . I guess they're okay."

"You're an Estorian. You've probably never made a fire, have you?"

Dominique blushed. "It's rude to watch the women work." *And even worse to do the work of women*, he thought. "Even when I was little my mother used to make me turn away for the lighting part."

"And you never peeked?"

Dominique turned bright pink. "Well, yes," he admitted. "But that was a long time ago. I hardly remember anything."

Riley snorted. "How do your men manage when they travel?

"Cicefyrian-wenches. Unmarried women who make the fires, cook . . ."

"Well, you are obviously not destined to be a

knight," Riley said with a haughty sniff. "Allow me to demonstrate."

Dominique moved closer. Sir Riley gathered a pile of dried grasses and added some small twigs from his bundle. His plump fingers were surprisingly nimble and, with skill born of years of practice, he struck his piece of steel against the flint stone. On the third or fourth shower of sparks, the grass began to smoulder. The knight blew gently on the glowing embers, cupping his hands behind the fragile pile of fuel as a wisp of smoke rose towards the sky.

"Gently, right? Blow too hard and the whole thing will go out. Mark of an amateur, that is—blowing like a ruddy hurricane." His already round cheeks puffed out so it looked like he had two apples tucked inside. The flames licked at the tiny pile and he sat back on his heels, his face flushed, perspiration making his bulbous forehead glisten. "I'll put a few of my starter twigs in your sack—use them sparingly. Gather sticks at your camp tonight and dry them out beside your evening fire, like I'm doing with those, there."

He waved his arm towards the fire he had built earlier to heat the stew. It was dying down now, but still threw off quite a bit of heat. A heap of twigs dried at the edge of the fire. "Then add slightly bigger sticks—like these, here—these are good. Pebblenut wood burns clean and hot, though there aren't many pebblenut trees where you're going. Mountain scruff pine or fliggin bushes . . . they'll do in a pinch."

He balanced more sticks on the fire, layering them in alternating directions.

"Leave spaces for air but make sure the sticks

overlap so the flames can jump from one to the other. Understand? Good. It's not so hard, once you get the hang of it."

He stood and kicked dirt over the new fire, snuffing it out. Dominique felt a strange sadness when Riley extinguished the fire.

"Pliny! Pliiiiny! You really must pack up, boy. You have a long way to go. Stop standing there staring at the dirt."

The knight kicked earth over the other fire. "Usually I'd douse it with water first, but I'm not keen about getting too close to the river."

Dominique nodded his agreement as he pulled his clothes back on. They were still slightly damp but much better than when he had crawled out of them before lunch.

Heee-anh!

Dominique jumped and then laughed as a small brown donkey ambled up to Sir Riley. Pliny waggled his oversized ears back and forth at Dominique. Navina whistled and flew down to sit on Dominique's shoulder. She chattered at Pliny and raised her wings to make herself look bigger.

Sir Riley laughed. "Pliny, my dear friend. Meet Dominique Elnedo—an Estorian who cannot tell stories."

The donkey brayed again, eliciting another volley of whistles and peeps from Dominique's bird.

Sir Riley chuckled to himself as he loaded his gear into two wicker panniers fastened to the donkey's sides.

"So, you're going to Carnillo now?" Dominique

asked as he stuffed his feather tunic back into his own sack.

"Aye."

"Alone?"

"I have Pliny. And a few tricks to keep me safe."

Riley tightened a strap holding one of the panniers closed. He fastened his sword to his side and then, from the second pannier, he pulled a long, brown robe. Sir Riley slipped the loose garment over his shirt and then exchanged his leather boots for a pair of rope sandals. Dominique recognized the sandals as the kind worn by roaming monks. One had visited the healing women of his band once, after the holy man had suffered a nasty fall from a windmill.

"What do you think?" Riley asked, waving a sturdy wooden staff at Dominique. A cluster of great soldiro feathers tied to the handle fluttered lightly in the breeze. If Riley had been an unlikely-looking knight before, he was completely disguised now.

"Perfect! I would believe you were a monk."

"Can't be too careful," Riley said, suddenly grave. "There are rumours of trouble—of an invasion from the mainland. Many people will speak to a monk who will not speak to a knight, even an old, fat knight like me."

His grin was back as he tucked the rest of his chain-mail armour into the baskets. The donkey sighed with the addition of the extra weight.

"Ready, handsome?"

"Yes, sir."

"I was actually talking to Pliny here. Ah, what a fine shade of radish red! Never mind. You're not the first to find it odd a man would speak to an ass as if he were a dear friend." He winked. "Good luck on your travels. And remember, underground or under cover before nightfall. Death by incubus must be the worst way to go!"

Dominique swallowed and looked up into the sky as if he might see an incubus hovering there.

"How *do* they do it—kill you, I mean."

Sir Riley gaped. "You don't know?" He rolled his eyes and clutched his hands over his chest. "They say having an incubus wrap around you is a waking nightmare, worse than dying. Incubus have no mercy and there's no way to fight them off. They fly on black wings as light and fragile as the wind. They wrap around you like a mist, seep inside you with every breath you try to draw until only the evil, poisonous form of the incubus fills your dying lungs. Once that happens, the incubus eats your body from the inside out, leaving only a withered shell behind."

Sir Riley wiped his palms across the great mound of his stomach. "I do not envy your journey," he said.

Dominique looked back at the river and then to the mountains ahead. Navina rubbed her head against his neck and tutted softly.

"The best of luck to you. Perhaps our paths will cross again."

"Yes, sir. And thank you for everything, sir."

"Indeed."

With that, the round knight in monk's clothing and his sturdy donkey set off towards the south, following the trail along the River Epilobium.

18

THE FALL

Tara listened for stories carried on the westerly winds. When she heard the call of spring, she moved her people from the caves of Ranginoor to the heart of the Festerworlds.

"I guess we'd better move on," Dominique said. Navina answered with a ruffle of feathers and a half-hearted chirp.

At first, the going was easy and he fell into a smooth, sweeping stride, swishing through the lush spring grasses, the sun warm on his back.

Several times he paused to watch the graceful arcs of eagles soaring high above. When the shadows of the big birds of prey floated over them, Navina hunkered down and pressed her head into the hollow between Dominique's chin and throat.

"Don't worry. They're not looking for you. Are you sure you don't want to fly a bit?"

At this suggestion the little bird gripped Dominique's shoulder so tightly, he winced as her claws pinched right through his shirt into his skin.

"Ow!" he complained, but he stopped trying to make Navina fly.

"That's where we're going," he said, his gaze fixed on the tall pillar of stone just visible on the side of Rain Mountain. "It's so quiet," he said, glancing around as if someone might be listening. Dominique started humming some of the old marching songs to himself, those he had heard whenever Protector Bertolescu's clan had moved from one encampment to another.

After two or three hours his voice was hoarse, his throat tight with thirst. He stopped singing and tried to push away his growing uneasiness. What he needed was a plan, something more useful than *keep going*.

Navina, too, seemed restless and unhappy. She paced back and forth on his shoulder, sometimes squatting as if to launch into the air, but never actually taking off. Dominique scanned the horizon but nothing moved except the grasses waving lazily before the wind. Navina peeped twice and started hopping from foot to foot, clearly agitated.

"What is the matter with you? Do you see another rabbit? A grass snake?"

Dominique picked up the bird. She stepped onto his finger and clutched it tightly when he offered it to her, but her gaze remained fixed on a point in the distance.

With a flash of red as her crest bobbed forward

and then flattened against the top of her head, Navina leaped from his finger and flew off.

Dominique scrambled after her, climbing a nearby knoll. He shielded his eyes and drew in a sharp breath. He squinted at two small dots moving along the foot of the mountains. It was someone on horseback who was leading a second horse behind, someone wearing a billowing black cloak.

"The Campriano," he whispered with a mix of disgust and a longing so strong he was shocked by it. He watched as the two horses disappeared into a fold in the mountains.

"Just as well he's so far away," Dominique said, but his voice quavered as he spoke and inside he fought an intense and fruitless longing to run and call after the stranger. He wanted to beg to be allowed to travel with the man. Campriano or not, it would be better than the terrible silence, the aching sadness of being alone.

Standing on the knoll, watching the spot where the traveller had slipped away into a hidden valley, a hideous dread seeped into Dominique's legs, numbing them, making it impossible to move.

He would never survive a whole year of this.

In that moment, as the full impact of all that had happened hit him, the foreboding that had taken hold of his legs now poured into his veins. The chill circulated through him, a paralyzing misery permeating his whole body.

Snippets of the Tara stories whirled through his head, old familiar tales told in the voices of his mother and aunts. These mixed with images of the

Stories he had heard from the other boys and men.

And when the stories came to Tara, she gathered her handmaidens on the beaches of Tanga and the listeners drew close. A gust of wind ruffled Dominique's hair. *And so, the boys learned never to walk alone. . . . After that, the Estorian women always fetched water in groups of three. . . .*

Dominique scanned the landscape for any sign of Navina. *The beautiful Shayla became the first cicefyrian-wench. She accompanied the great Bronio Zeldon when he visited the King of High Chestonia to tell stories of the distant revolution. His tales saved the lives of thousands of Chestonian citizens, and ever since, Estorians and their cicefyrian-wenches have been welcomed to the kingdom.*

"Navina!"

Navina whistled sharply, announcing her return with a whir of wings.

"Don't ever do that again!" he shouted. "Don't ever leave me!" Shaking, he lifted the bird close to his lips and blew gently on the back of her neck, ruffling the little feathers.

How pathetic. He had nobody but a bird for company, unless he counted the deerskin sack that bump-a-bumped against his back as he walked. Dominique blinked hard, trying to clear the tears from his eyes. They trickled down his cheeks and soon his shoulders heaved with great miserable sobs and his nose dripped. Navina nibbled at his cheek, but he couldn't be comforted.

Dominique stumbled forward, half running and half staggering. Inside, a great battle raged between his desire to continue and his equally strong longing to give in to his misery and collapse right there on the ground, to lie down and wait for hungry wild animals to devour him.

What did it matter if buzzards plucked out his eyes and red ants gnawed on his flesh? What difference would it make if a whole flock of incubus swooped down on him at nightfall and carried him away to their place of perpetual darkness? As he lurched along, Navina clung to his shoulder, whistling and peeping in alarm.

The thought of the incubus brought a fresh wave of dread and more tears, and he wailed his misery until his throat hurt and his eyes burned.

He was so wrapped in his own muffling blanket of grief that he didn't notice his lengthening shadow, or the warning mounds of soft earth. It wasn't until it was too late that the hideous stench of yagabono musk stung his nose and eyes and brought on a fresh wave of tears.

He had no time to react. Dominique tripped on a mound of earth and tumbled into a yagabono pit, sending Navina sailing off his shoulder with a terrified flurry of beating wings.

19

THE YAGABONO PIT

*Tibor hesitated at the fork in the road, unsure
which way to turn.*

Dominique yelped as he landed on his backside
deep inside the smelly pit. He struggled to his feet,
one hand reaching out to the dirt wall for support,
the other covering his nose and mouth in a futile
attempt to control the stink.

The stench was far worse than he could have
imagined from the warnings of others. The air was
so thick it caught in his throat, tore into the delicate
tissues of his nostrils. The pungent stench was as
bitter as burnt cabbage and as foul as the smell of
vomit. He clutched his stomach and struggled not to
heave its contents onto the ground.

Navina flew down into the hole, whistling
anxiously. She landed on Dominique's head and
shrieked sharp alarm cries. Doubled over, his eyes

streaming, Dominique waved her away. "Not now! I know it stinks!"

Navina tugged at Dominique's hair with her beak until Dominique opened his bleary eyes, still red and stinging from the acrid stench, to look at what was in the pit with him. Not more than two arm lengths away, on the other side of the pit, a vigorous-looking yagabono stood on its hind legs.

"Get away from me!" Dominique shouted, staggering backwards and crashing over a heap of giant clamshells. The yagabono peered down its long snout at Dominique, who lay absolutely still, panting. He ground his fists into his eyes, gasping. The animal's silver-tipped fur bristled and it snorted at the intruders.

Dominique decided to try a gentler approach and whispered, "Hello, friend. I won't hurt you." The animal's small ears twitched, but otherwise it remained motionless. Dominique rose slowly to his feet.

The yagabono's nostrils flared and its gaze shifted to the little bird.

"Sit still!" Dominique hissed at Navina, who hopped up and down on his head. "Easy," Dominique said to the yagabono. "Easy. It's all right."

The animal took a step forward and Dominique coughed and gagged as another wave of stink wafted towards him. The yagabono's huge front claws rested lightly on its broad chest, twitching.

"Navina, no! Stay still."

Scarlet crest blazing, the bird launched herself from

Dominique's head and flew straight at the yagabono.

"No!"

The yagabono's jaws snapped and a long trailing string of saliva swung from its lips. Navina darted behind the creature and sank her claws into the thick scruff of fur at the back of its neck. She hung on, shrieking, as the animal twisted back and forth, trying to shake her loose.

Frantically, Dominique scrabbled through the junk littered across the bottom of the pit. He needed a weapon. The animal swung its huge head from side to side, but it couldn't reach Navina, who clung to her safe spot behind it.

In the same moment, Dominique and the yagabono froze, listening to a strange deep clicking sound coming from Navina. The yagabono dropped slowly to all fours and lowered its head. Its small, round ears swivelled as it listened intently to the hollow tocking sounds coming from Navina's chest. Nearly as big as Dominique when it was standing upright, on all fours the yagabono was about the size of a white timber wolf. It snuffled and sighed and then dropped its chin to its paws.

"Good girl, Navina." With each tock, Navina's colours faded slightly. She didn't move, but stayed where she was, clinging to the ruff of thick fur. The yagabono looked no more harmful than a lazy dog.

"I'm not going to hurt you," Dominique said. "I'll just be climbing right out of—"

The creature's lips drew back to reveal a double row of rotting yellow and black teeth. Navina started another round of soothing noises and the yagabono half closed its eyes.

Dominique glanced above him and fought back another wave of tears as he saw just how deep the hole was. He lifted the edge of Bethusela's oversized cotton shift and pressed the fabric to his nose, drawing shallow breaths through his mouth so the smell was less intense.

Though it no longer seemed so agitated, the yagabono moved its head slowly from side to side, sniffing for the intruder's scent. With a gasp of horror, Dominique saw the huge effort it was taking for Navina to hold on to the massive beast and make the low, soothing noises that had lulled the animal into a sleepy stupor.

The colour was nearly gone from Navina's breast and her flight feathers were beginning to fade. Only once had Dominique seen a kasyapa bird paler than Navina was now.

"Navina. Let go. Fly away."

Navina kept making the strange noise. "Go now! Fly away!"

The tips of her tail feathers were pure white. Dominique leaned down and picked up a handful of pebbles. She could not become much paler before she would be too weak to fly away. Dominique aimed carefully and threw a pebble at Navina, knocking her off balance. She cried out in pain and relinquished her grip.

"Navina—I'm sorry."

The yagabono turned around, looking for the bird, and Dominique flung the rest of the stones at the yagabono's head.

With a yelp, the animal stopped and peered back at Dominique. Navina leaped into the air and flew out of the pit.

Dominique's heart raced. Navina had escaped but he was far from safe.

The yagabono took a step. "No! Get away from me." Dominique jumped up and down, waving his arms. He raised his closed fist as if he were going to throw something else, even though he had nothing in his hand. The animal stopped and its gaze shifted to a point somewhere above Dominique's head, outside the hole. A second later, a wild tonneck landed on top of the heap of freshly excavated dirt piled in the middle of the pit floor.

The tonneck, caught between the stares of Dominique and the yagabono, crouched in terror. Its sides puffed in and out and its nose quivered violently. The yagabono pounced, claws first, onto its prey.

With a quick twist, the yagabono broke the tonneck's neck and not two minutes later rested on its back legs, licking the last tonneck morsels from its thin, black lips with a quick sliver of pink tongue.

Dominique's knees buckled and he sank to the ground. "Navina . . ." he whispered. He couldn't call her back to become the yagabono's next meal.

The creature burped, stretched, and then turned its back on Dominique. It snuffled and began digging. The small space filled with grunts, snorts, and the sound of long claws scraping into the dirt walls of the pit. Warily, Dominique let out a long, slow breath and risked another longing look up at the pit opening far above.

The yagabono's head and shoulders had disappeared into a large hole in the opposite wall. After gouging out six or seven huge scoops of dirt, the yagabono thrust the soil backwards between its hind legs. It repeated this several times and then backed up to the heap of accumulated dirt, shaking mud from its thick ruff of fur. With a mighty heave of its webbed back feet it sent the whole pile flying backwards, up and out of the pit.

"Yeuch." Dominique spat out a stray lump of grit and shifted over slightly so he was out of the line of fire. The yagabono resumed digging and a fresh pile of dirt grew in the middle of the pit.

The walls of the pit reached higher than the tips of Dominique's fingers if he stretched as tall as he could. Beyond the sharp edges of the hole, the sky was deepening in colour. The incubus were out there somewhere. Even if he could somehow escape from this pit, there was no time to find an abandoned one to hide in before dark.

A wave of nausea threatened to overwhelm him when Dominique sniffed cautiously to see if he was getting used to the awful smell.

Well, Dominique decided, if he was going to stay, he'd better find a way to defend himself. A few heavy stones lay on the ground and several more were half covered with dirt. Dominique gathered these on a big pile, ready to heave them at the yagabono should it attack. Each time the digging creature backed up to clear the pit of loose dirt,

Dominique spoke to it.

"You don't want to eat me, do you? I'm too big, right? I throw things."

A series of grunts was the only reply. The yagabono squeezed back into the hole and struggled to tunnel around something stubborn, a root or a stone. After a time it stopped digging, backed up to the excavated dirt, pushed its back feet under the pile, and repeated its kicking handstand. The loose dirt sailed up and out of the pit.

"Why don't you kick me out like that?" Dominique wished aloud and put his hand protectively on his rock pile. It seemed a pathetic defence. Maybe there was something better in the debris littering the ground. The bottom of the pit was covered not just with heaps of dirt, but bits and pieces of metal, fabric, feathers, twine, bones, and shards of pottery. There had to be something he could use to escape.

Keeping an eye on the back end of the burrowing animal, Dominique tugged at a bit of string trailing out from under some conch shells, each one nearly the size of his head. The string, which Dominique thought might be useful to slip into his bag, wouldn't come free. Quietly, he reached for his bag and felt around inside for the small knife. He couldn't find it. Dominique tipped the bag upside down and shook it.

His feather tunic, the bundle of sticks, and his package of rice fell out into his lap. He shook the bag again but there was nothing else inside.

"Where is my . . ." His face flushed when he

turned the bag inside out and realized his knife, fish hooks, candle, and blanket were all gone. His stomach knotted. Sir Riley must have helped himself when he had tucked the fire sticks into Dominique's bag.

Dominique clenched his jaw with helpless fury. Checking each interior pocket carefully, he discovered his fire-starting flint and nothing else. *How nice of Riley to leave me sticks and fire-starter*, he thought bitterly. How could Sir Riley have taken his things? Could there be a hole in the sack? Dominique blinked hard and searched again. There was no hole.

He reached up to his shoulder to find comfort in stroking his bird, but Navina wasn't there. He whistled, but there was no answering call from beyond the edge of the pit. Was she all right? Had he hurt her badly with the stone? What if he'd killed her? No, he couldn't have. She had flown away. The stone had been small and he'd only thrown it to save her. She had been fading. . . . Dominique squelched a small gasp of grief. *She'll be waiting for me outside*, he tried to reassure himself.

He tugged again at the end of the string and pulled it free. It wasn't actually a string at all but the edge of a fishing net buried under the rubble in the pit. Carefully, one tentative tug at a time, he pulled the net towards him.

As the darkness deepened, it became harder and harder to see anything. Dominique stopped pulling in case the other end was where the yagabono was digging.

In the pitch blackness the snorting and snuffling

seemed three times louder than before, but to Dominique's relief the noises didn't seem to be coming any closer. Outside, the sound of the wind grew louder and Dominique shivered.

Groping around near his feet, he found his feather tunic where it had fallen from the sack. He pulled it on over his cotton shift, drew his knees close to his chest, and slumped against the dirt wall behind him.

Exhaustion made every bone in his body ache. Sleep, though, was too dangerous. Determined to stay awake, Dominique began to chant marching songs under his breath.

When the land was dark, we marched from fear. . . .

CHAPTER

20

THE RING

"Take this ring," the king said, "and when you find yourself in a spot of trouble, kiss it thrice."

The cool grey light of pre-dawn filtered into the pit and Dominique jerked awake.

Fragments of dreams muddied his thinking—images of running across a wide field, wings tied to his arms, his arms flapping wildly as if he could take off, a strange kind of fog swirling through the midsection of a yagabono that was tangled in a fishing net.

Rubbing his fists into his eyes, Dominique sat up properly. Judging by the dull buzz in his head, he couldn't have slept long.

He wasn't the only one snoozing. On the other side of the pit, the yagabono lay curled into a tight ball, snoring softly. Dominique's stomach rumbled. His hand closed on a bone and he raised its gristly end halfway to his mouth before he let it fall uneaten to the ground.

He ran his tongue across his parched lips. They were dry and cracked and his tongue felt as if it were coated with some thick, unpleasant stickiness. Peering up at the square of pale blue sky above him, Dominique thought, *No rain today.*

So, this was how he was going to die—not beneath the Protector's sword, but in a smelly hole filled with rubbish and a sleeping yagabono.

He could try to light a fire. The other traveller, the Campriano, might see it and come to rescue him. Maybe Navina had gone for help. Maybe someone was already on the way. Sir Riley? Dominique's eyes narrowed. Perhaps he was better off not being rescued by the likes of Riley. If a knight of honour could rob him, what might a Campriano do? Slit his throat and leave his body to rot in the stinking pit? "You'd have a great meal then, wouldn't you?" he whispered to the yagabono.

Dominique studied the creature as it stretched in its sleep and rolled onto its back. Its massive front claws scrabbled in the air and its muzzle twitched. Dominique could just make out the slightly darker line of the fold of skin at the top edge of the pouch on its belly.

So, you're a female, he thought, hoping her mate wasn't due for a visit. The yagabonos were generally solitary animals that only sought out company during the mating season. Though nobody from Dominique's family had ever crossed the River

Epilobium, Dominique remembered a couple of the grandfathers telling stories about the odd marsupials of the high plains.

They were like crows, the way they collected odds and ends and took them back to their lairs. They didn't restrict themselves to small, shiny objects, though—they collected anything that could be stuffed into their generous pouches. Now, looking at the soft, white fur of the yagabono's underbelly, Dominique noticed that the pouch was not empty.

A smooth rim of some sort eased in and out of the pouch as the animal breathed. A dish? Too small. Dominique eased himself forward until he was close enough to see that the thing was some sort of disc or ring about the size of his fist and very ornate.

The yagabono grunted in its sleep and Dominique scuttled back. The animal's powerful hind legs, so good at kicking dirt up and out of the hole, were relaxed, and as the creature slept on, Dominique had a good chance to study the strange webbed back feet and powerful haunches. He imagined the ease with which the creature could leap out of its pit and bound off across the grasslands. If only he could do the same. . . .

As he sat, idly fiddling with the edge of the fishing net, Dominique's forehead creased as he thought again of his dream of a yagabono tangled in a fishing net. A surge of excitement sent a tingle down his spine. His hands were suddenly all thumbs as he pulled the rest of the net free.

The net was an old one and not in very good shape. Though the rope tied along the top edge seemed strong enough, the rest of the net had several holes in it. With shaking hands he pulled the sides of one of the holes wide open. Holding his breath and being careful not to trip on anything, Dominique crept closer to the yagabono's hind feet. Very gently, he slipped the hole in the net over one of the animal's back legs and slowly, ever so slowly, tightened some of the loose strings. Soon the net was snugged in place and Dominique backed away.

"Navina!" Dominique's delight at seeing Navina, her plumage bright as it had ever been, was quickly replaced with alarm. "Go away!" What a time for the bird to return. She circled with wild wingbeats, banking sharply so she didn't hit the pit walls.

The yagabono's head jerked up and its little black eyes peered shortsightedly this way and that. Startled, Dominique jumped backwards. The creature leaped up, swatting at Navina.

"Watch out!"

Navina darted close to the yagabono's snapping jaws, whistling and calling and flapping her wings madly.

The yagabono tensed her mighty back legs, and Dominique screamed, "Go! Fly away!"

Navina pounded the air with her wings, darting this way and that just out of reach. She scrambled up and out of the pit. With a single, powerful leap and a nasty snarl, the beast followed her, the net slithering along behind.

Dominique pounced on the net as it flew past

him, twisting his left hand into the web of tight knots before the yagabono hit the other end. Dominique staggered, trying to stay on his feet. The strong hemp cord bit into the soft flesh of his wrist. The yagabono answered the pull at her back leg with a roar of rage and fear and flung herself at the other end of the net. Dominique jumped up at the wall, scrabbling to find a toehold. As he inched his way up, the yagabono threw herself at the end of the net again and again, inadvertently pulling Dominique towards freedom.

The rope sawed into Dominique's wrist and he screamed again. With his free hand he felt the top edge of the hole, and with a huge effort he flung himself onto the grass outside.

The yagabono chose that moment to turn and flee. With each great leap she soared three or four metres. Dominique slammed into the ground. He struggled to his feet and tried to free his wrist, but the crazed creature bounded ahead, keeping the net taut. With each bounce, the cord wrapped tighter and yanked Dominique forward. He fought to keep his footing as he flew along behind the yagabono screaming, "Stop!"

The creature, reacting to the muddy boy screeching and waving his free arm, redoubled her efforts to escape until Dominique tripped again and thudded into the ground with a soft *oof*. This time, he didn't get up.

The yagabono wrenched and pulled, trying to drag the weight along the ground. Dominique cried out, pleading for the enraged animal to stop yanking his twisted arm, until his parched throat ached. Then, without warning, the fierce tugging stopped. Cautiously, Dominique lifted his head. The yagabono had turned around and was gnawing away at the offending net now tightly wrapped around its back leg. Dominique felt a twinge of guilt, but only until pieces of the net fell away and the yagabono shook herself free and bounded away across the grasslands.

Dominique lay in the grass battered and exhausted, his face contorted with pain. With a flutter, Navina landed on his shoulder. She pecked and tugged at his ear.

"I can't move. I can't . . ."

Navina took several strands of hair and pulled.

"Ow! Stop that. I'll . . . I'll sit up."

Dominique cradled his wounded arm in his lap and gingerly worked the tight cords loose. Underneath, the skin was raw and bleeding. The arm felt as if it had been stretched to twice its normal length and he was a little surprised it was still attached to his body at all.

He moaned. His lips and tongue were swollen and dry beyond belief. Navina landed a short distance away and hopped back and forth. Seeing he wasn't moving, she flew back to him, pecked at his cheek, and then flew away again.

"I can't follow you," he whispered. At this, the bird fluttered towards him, again landing just out of reach in front of him. He lunged towards her, flinching as his injured hand moved. He fell forward and collapsed, his cheek pressed into the grass.

Beside herself with distress, Navina hopped onto Dominique's head and grabbed hold of his ear. She nipped at his soft earlobe and bit down as hard as she could.

"Ow!" He batted her away. "What are you doing?" She flew a little way ahead again and he staggered to his feet, trying to follow her. "What is that?" he asked, bending down to see what she was standing on. He picked up a wooden ring big enough to fit easily over his hand and about as thick as his thumb.

He recognized the ring as the thing from the yagabono's pouch. Dominique turned it over, admiring the figures and symbols carved into the wood. Slipping it onto his uninjured wrist, Dominique was disappointed that it didn't fit. It was much too big.

He sat down and pulled at it to see if it would stretch. Maybe he could wear it around his neck.

"Oh, no—it broke."

But the ring wasn't broken at all. It had pulled apart into two halves, but when Dominique fiddled with the two parts they slipped back together and clicked into place.

He pulled the ring in half again and clicked it back together around his ankle, where he wouldn't lose it.

He stood, swaying, and turned to face the mountains. The land sloped gently away from him up towards the foothills rolling like big, green waves into the grey base of the mountains.

Up there, somewhere, was water. But where?

WATER

*Blinta hopped down from the stump, holding
the golden goblet tightly. The inscription was
clear enough: "Die trying."*

Navina flew back to him and perched on his
shoulder. "Navina, maybe we should go back."

But Lagrace waited at the river. Navina clicked
her beak and whistled.

"Shh. I know, I know." Dominique tickled
Navina's favourite spot at the back of her neck. "I
wouldn't be able to resist the music now."

He picked up his sack and winced, his arm
throbbing. "The boy set off towards the east," he
said, repeating part of Tibor's story.

"The boy set off. . . ."

Looking down at his toes, they seemed impos-
sibly far away, as if his feet didn't even belong to
him. If they weren't his, he couldn't tell them what

to do. That was ridiculous. Of course his feet belonged to him.

"Move."

Dominique watched his knee bend and lift and he stumbled forward.

"Keep going. Left. Right. Go. Go."

Lie down. Lie down, the grasses whispered, bobbing their heads and beckoning to Dominique.

"Right. Left."

Come. Rest.

"Step. Step."

Rest. Rest.

Navina whistled and ruffled her feathers and Dominique turned his head to see her watching him. All he managed was a hoarse whisper.

"No. I won't rest. Not yet."

Dominique pushed his tongue between his lips but couldn't lick them because his mouth was so dry.

"Walk. Walk." His feet plodded on.

With each step, Navina peeped softly close to Dominique's ear. The voices of the grandfathers murmured, competing with the plaintive calls of the soft grasses.

The difficulties were many and the journey harsh. . . ."

Dominique's lips twisted into a raw grin. So that's what the old Storytellers meant.

Every so often he lifted his gaze and tried to judge his progress towards the distant mountains. The distinctive projection of the tusk wasn't coming any closer.

"Twenty more steps," he said. "Twenty steps and then we'll rest. One . . . two . . . three . . . keep going. Don't sit down yet. Eighteen . . . move. Nineteen . . . step. Twenty." He rested for a count of twenty and forced himself to move on again.

As he picked his way across the plain, Navina stuck close by. Sometimes she flew a short distance ahead, but most of the time she remained perched on his shoulder, clucking, chirping, and whistling.

"Sixteen . . . walk . . . seventeen . . . step . . . eight—what? Stop picking at my ear. What is the matter with you?"

Dominique looked towards the ridge where Navina stared, intent and rigid. A glint of sunshine caught in something shiny and then was gone.

Dominique swiped at his eyes with the back of his hand and blinked, but the distant wall of stone was smooth, unbroken. Nothing moved.

The boy Tibor stayed so long in the wilds without water, he saw light where there was no light, and water where there was no water.

"Hey! Come back!" Navina didn't listen. She swept low over the grass, over a hillock, and out of sight. Counting forgotten, Dominique ran forward. The wind hissed through the grasses and whirled around him, tossing his hair into his eyes, slapping the tatty edge of the shift against his thighs.

"Navina!" He stopped, held his breath, and listened for a whistle. What he heard instead was the trickle of water. Dominique's leaden legs moved of their own accord and a moment later he fell to his knees beside a small stream. The water gurgled

174

its way through a narrow channel carved in the plain. Navina hopped in and out of a shallow puddle, spraying water droplets up over her back with a flurry of wings.

"Mmmm."

Using his good arm, Dominique splashed his face and drank, drawing the cool, sparkling water over his tongue. He rinsed the caked mud off his arms and legs and cleaned his wounds as best he could, and then drank some more. He plunged his face into the stream and splashed water through his hair and over the back of his neck, still prickling hot from the relentless sun, before drinking again.

When, at last, he had slaked his thirst, he rocked back on his heels and watched Navina pulling each long flight feather through her hooked beak.

"How about something to eat, my little Navina?" He stomped a circle in the grass, flattening the stalks until he had a comfortable place to sit. In the middle of the level area he scraped the grass away completely so he could build his fire in the dirt. Dominique pulled the kindling bundle from his sack and criss-crossed the twigs over each other the way Riley had shown him.

"Come on, light." Dominique puffed gently at the tiny fire licking hungrily at the kindling. *Stupid Riley.*

Dominique tipped his rice into Bethusela's stew pot, added water, and hurried back to the fire. It was nearly out.

More wood. He needed to find more wood— and quickly. He scanned the surrounding plain. The nearest tree, a gnarled snag, was way off in the distance, too far away to get there and back before the fire went out.

Grass might burn. He pulled a handful of chin-chin grass and dropped it on the fire. Fresh and green, the grass melted and smoked but didn't burn. Pushing the tall, new growth aside, he tore out a clump of the previous year's dead and crispy grass and added it to the smouldering heap.

Blow gently, he admonished himself when his first, enthusiastic blast nearly extinguished the flame.

The dried grass caught, flared up briefly, and then the fire threatened to die out completely.

"What do I do?" he asked Navina. "There's nothing to burn." Navina, snacking on chin-chin seeds, paid no attention.

Dominique's stomach rumbled and he threw several more handfuls of dry chin-chin on the fire and kicked his way through the grass, hoping to find a stray bit of wood that he might burn. What his foot sent flying was not a stick but a lump of dung about the size of a bowl. It lifted easily into the air in one piece and then plopped back down a short distance away.

Dominique bent over the heap of scat and inspected it. Bear? Wrong shape. Definitely not deer or tonneck—those were pebbly, and this was more like a festival flatcake.

He glanced around, half expecting to see a herd of large creatures swarming around him, though he realized that was silly. The dung was quite dry, very old, and had no odour whatsoever. Probably not yagabono. Besides, the yagabono probably buried theirs, he decided, since they were such good diggers.

His belly grumbled again.

Would dried dung burn?

He broke off a couple of pieces and fed the tiny flames. The dung burned well—slowly and evenly, if a little smokily. A quick search turned up a number of similar piles and soon he had quite a collection gathered by the fire.

I can do this, he thought. He had water and fire—he could manage.

Dominique nestled the pot of rice and beans into the fire and wiped a little trickle of drool from the corner of his mouth with the back of his hand. Sheepishly, he looked over his shoulder. It was a good thing his mother wasn't watching. He stifled a pang of sadness. He wished his mother *were* there to scold him.

Don't think of her, he told himself sternly. *Think of . . . dung. More dung*. He hurried away, scooping up more fuel for his fire, scolding himself as he went. He needed to pay attention, keep the fire stoked, and find a good stick to stir the rice so it didn't stick to the pot.

When the rice was finally soft enough to eat, he fell upon his meal like a wild animal, blowing on each mouthful he scooped from the pot so that he didn't burn his tongue.

Navina flitted through the grasses, nibbling at the delicate new shoots, the same vivid green as the underside of her wings.

It wasn't long before Dominique was licking out the inside of the bowl, determined to get every last grain. His belly full, he lay down beside the stream and rested as he contemplated the best route to take.

The stream meandered into the foothills, and Dominique assumed it originated somewhere up in the mountains. Even though it seemed to head in a direction a little too far south of the tusk to be able to follow it all the way to his destination, he decided that having a ready water supply was worth the slightly longer route.

"Do we have to move?" he asked Navina. His whole body screamed in protest. The little bird hopped onto his head and gently pulled two or three hairs at a time through her beak. She made a soft clicking sound as she preened, and Dominique relaxed into the grass. How wonderful it would be to just lie back and rest, to catch up on the sleep he had missed the night before, to allow his aching body some time to recover.

"Ow! Ow, stop!" Navina grasped a strand of hair in her beak and yanked. "I'm not sleeping!" he said, rubbing his eyes and yawning. Navina kept on pulling until Dominique rose to his knees, waving his hand at her. "Stop it! We'll keep going. Let go!"

Dominique gathered his things, put out the fire, and grumbled a string of complaints at his colourful companion.

As they travelled towards the mountains, the hills grew larger. The stream wound its way along through the gullies and dips between the hills. After a while, the landscape became more rugged and the yagabono pits less frequent. Soon it was rare for Dominique to see the telltale mounds of dirt or to catch a whiff of a pit inhabitant.

Because he spent most of his time picking his way along the valley bottoms, he often lost sight of the tusk. Every so often he scrambled up to the top of one of the hills to get his bearings.

It was late in the afternoon during one of these excursions when he struggled, panting with exertion, to the top of a particularly rocky rise. From there he saw three creatures grazing on top of the next hill. He dropped to his stomach and flattened himself to the ground, fighting to slow his breathing so he wouldn't be heard.

Lifting his head only high enough to see over the grass, Dominique watched the animals slowly making their way along the crest of the hill.

"Leranons," Dominique whispered. The animals were beautiful. Every few mouthfuls of grass they raised white heads and looked around. Their ears flicked back and forth, relaxed but alert to any danger. The stories were right.

And the great creatures were the picture of dignity. But when Lord Anagal challenged the leader, the beast ran him through and left him for dead.

From the middle of each of their foreheads a long white horn speared the air. Though their forelegs were like those of horses, where the animals' withers would normally have been, their coats began to change colour from the snowy white of the head, neck, and mane to a tawny brown. The hindquarters of the creatures were lion-like and as they grazed, their long, feline tails swished from side to side just above the grass.

The largest of the leranons lifted its head and stopped chewing. It looked straight at the spot where Dominique lay hidden. Dominique pressed himself closer to the ground, the rich smells of sun-warmed earth filling his nostrils, his whole body tense with listening and fear.

After what seemed like ages of lying motionless, Dominique dared to look again. The animals had moved farther along the ridge. As he watched, the largest leranon looked back in his direction and this time stamped his hoof. Then, all together, the three magnificent creatures shrugged and shook their shoulders and backs, like great dogs ridding themselves of water. As Dominique watched, the animals shuddered and wings unfolded from their sides. With powerful cat leaps, they sprang up into the air. Graceful for such large creatures, they circled once and then winged their way east towards the mountains.

CAPTURE

*When he awoke, he was a prisoner in their
black cave, surrounded by stone walls wet with
the blood of innocent victims, air filled with the
cries of lost souls.*

Dominique stayed where he was, afraid to move in
case the flying horse-lions came back. There were
so many stories of leranons and their prisoners, like
the horrible tale of Polento the Innocent.

*Polento left his clan when food became so
scarce his people began dying.*

According to the story, Polento's plan was to
travel to the Valley of Abundance, where he would
tell his most beautiful Story of the Rainbow Children
in exchange for baskets of juicy kelba fruit and
sacks of sweet ronen flour.

*Polento never reached the Valley of Abundance
for he was a lazy man at heart and lay down in the*

tall summer grasses for many rests. Dominique's eyes drifted closed as the words of the Story echoed on in his mind, familiar and comforting. *The leranons captured him as he slept and carried him away. When he awoke, he was a prisoner in their black cave, surrounded by stone walls wet with the blood of innocent victims, air filled with the cries of lost souls.*

Dominique slept fitfully, half aware of Navina trying everything she could to wake him, as the sun dropped below the horizon and the air grew chilly. Once darkness had fallen, each whisper and sigh of the wind echoed the eerie calls of the incubus. The rising breeze ruffled Dominique's hair, but though he felt Navina running back and forth over his shoulders, Dominique could not rouse himself to move on. The wind moaned as if it, too, were trying to warn Dominique. Navina raised her wings and beat them mightily as she let out a series of desperate warning whistles. Her terrified shrieks finally pierced the cloak of his unconsciousness and he stirred and tried to sit up.

Dominique didn't have a chance to fully awaken because just then a whoosh and swirl of ice blackness descended around his head like a stifling cloak.

He threw up his hands to ward off the smothering force of the incubus. For a terrifying moment he teetered back and forth between waking and oblivion. Flailing wildly, he crashed backwards into blackness.

Dominique waved feebly at the black air before his face, struggling against the fierce pain in his chest, fighting to breathe, to pull in even the smallest of breaths.

So, this was it—he was going to cross the Jade Bridge, his insides dried out and swallowed up by a marauding incubus. Dominique's heart thudded until he thought it would burst from behind his ribs in a violent, bloody explosion. He tried to cry out, but no sound escaped his lips. He closed his eyes and struck out madly at the air in front of him. He was at the place where Stories ended, alone at the final moment, even his bird gone.

And then, the impossible happened. He drew a breath—not a large one, but a breath nonetheless. What was happening? Was the incubus resting? Was he already dead? Dominique's heart raced faster and he took another sip of air, then another, and then heaved a shuddering sigh of relief. The thing, the incubus must have gone!

Dominique opened his eyes and this time when he screamed the sound split the night. A massive body loomed between him and the stars above. Warm breath puffed moist against his cheek. This was not the cold, life-sucking chill of the incubus. This was some sort of huge animal with breath as sweet as clover.

"Travelenum mysteria," a deep voice murmured close to Dominique's ear.

"Campriano?" asked someone else close by.

The first creature lowered its massive head close to the ground and sniffed at Dominique. The tip of its long, single horn pressed into the ground so close to his head he could feel the ridges along its length brushing against his ear.

Leranons! At least two of them.

"Ni Campriano. Despicalo! Yagabono-bis."

The leranon tilted his head to the side, his horn still pressed to the earth. Vague, shadowy forms swept back and forth behind and above him, hissing and whispering. The leranon shook out its wings, making a canopy to shield Dominique. When the creature spoke again its deep voice darkened with concern.

"Incubus mordeno-wel." The two animals were joined by a third who shouted something in Leranese. The three of them began to debate in earnest. Unable to move, pinned to the ground between the great beast's hooves, Dominique could catch only a few words, and those he only half understood.

"Traitorio . . ."

". . . Campriano . . ."

". . . despicalo . . ."

"Incubus . . . temporo minesculo."

The animals seemed to be arguing, and as they did, the dark shapes swooping through the air came closer and closer, forcing the sheltering wings of the leranon to dip down towards the earth.

"Angloise?" one of the other voices asked.

"Yes. Yes!" Dominique could manage no words beyond this.

"We feel your fear," said the first leranon, his muzzle close to Dominique's ear. "The incubus close are."

Dominique shuddered, chilled to the bone. His limbs seemed heavy, thick.

"We take you from here."

He couldn't resist the firm command in the animal's voice. A few more words were exchanged in rapid Leranese. Then a second leranon moved

184

until he was standing behind Dominique's head. He pushed his muzzle at Dominique's side. The third leranon's horn prodded at him until, woozy with terror, Dominique sat up and allowed himself to be nudged to his feet.

"Get on. We fly now."

The second leranon leaped into the air and hovered over the first, his wings beating rapidly, ruffling Dominique's hair with each downdraft.

"Be fast!" shouted the third leranon, who circled above them, stirring the air with his great wings and creating whirlpools that twisted and turned the dark shadows of the incubus in confused spirals.

"Put your feet forward. I must my wings open. Good. Now, hold on." Dominique wrapped the fingers of his good arm into the thick, white mane and braced himself. The powerful haunches of Dominique's mount kicked out, launching them into the air. Nothing could have prepared him for the powerful thrust as the animal leaped. At the same time, the leranon gave a great shudder and shook his huge wings open.

"Navina!" Dominique shrieked. In a wild moment of panic he looked at the receding ground. Should he leap for safety? Escape from his captors? Where was Navina?

A soft clicking came from the deerskin bag he clutched to his chest with his injured arm. He could barely hear the sound over the roar of the wind in his ears, the shouts of the leranons, and the furious screeches of the incubus.

"Navina!" he whispered in response. Something

small and warm shifted inside the bag.

"Altitudeno!" one of the leranons called. All three of the massive flying creatures banked sharply to the right and climbed higher and higher until Dominique's face was wet with mist and wisps of low clouds obscured the other leranons.

"My leg!" Dominique screamed when bony claws grasped at his ankle.

"Hold on!" his rescuer said as he redoubled his efforts to fly high out of reach of the incubus. "Anwar! Help!"

With each powerful wingbeat the leranon grunted and Dominique's head snapped back. Ignoring the burning pain in his arm, he held on to his bag and clenched his fingers more tightly in the leranon's mane.

"It's got me!" Dominique screamed as the claws of the incubus sank deeper into his ankle.

A second leranon dived towards them, his horn pointed at the winged shadow clutching at Dominique's foot. The vicious thrust nearly unseated him. The piercing wail of the incubus careening away into space made the hairs at the back of Dominique's neck stand straight up. From inside the bag he heard Navina's terrified peeps but could offer her no comfort.

Then, there was silence except for the panting of the three leranons as they burst through the low clouds and into the clean blackness of night air untroubled by demons.

CHAPTER
23

FLIGHT

*Once captured, there was nothing the boy
could do but touch the ring in his pocket and
hope the great king would hear his pleas for
mercy.*

It didn't take long before Dominique was used to
the jerkiness of leranon flight. At first, he counted
wing strokes to try to estimate how long they had
been aloft, but he gave up after reaching more than
three hundred. He wondered how far they were
going but didn't dare shift his position for fear of
slipping from his perch astride the great winged
beast. His arm ached and his ankle burned and
throbbed, but he couldn't risk loosening his grip on
the deerskin sack or he would never see Navina
again.

"Ohh," he groaned, the strain of holding on
sending pains shooting up his good arm. The leranons

banked sharply to the left and began to descend. Now that the moon had risen, Dominique could see reasonably well. The high, shadowy forms of the mountains loomed around them, so close it seemed the leranons' wingtips were dragging across the faces of the surrounding cliffs.

With a clatter of loose stones, the three animals landed on a small plateau surrounded on all sides by wide chasms. Dominique's mount's sides rose and fell as the leranon struggled to catch his breath.

Dominique shivered violently. "Do I have time to put on my tunic?" he asked in a small voice. One of the leranons nodded.

The three animals conferred quietly in Leranese as Dominique found his feather tunic and pulled it awkwardly over his head.

"Get down." The big leranon kneeled and Dominique scrambled off its back. *Just do as they say*, he told himself.

"Anwar will speak. His Angloise best."

A second leranon lowered his head until his horn pointed straight at Dominique's chest. Dominique took a step backwards.

"Camprianos not welcome in our lands," Anwar said, his voice cold and even.

"But—"

"Quiet. Many years your people set traps, hunt us, capture our strongest, make us work as slaves."

"No! We—"

"Be still." Anwar advanced so the tip of his horn nudged Dominique's breastbone. Dominique took another step backwards, closer to the edge of the cliff.

"We not save you from the incubus because we like you," Anwar continued.

"No, I didn't think so. But, thank you. Thank you—that was very brave."

"We take you back to Carnillo alive if you help us make free the leranons your people take away in this winter."

Dominique's heart dropped. So that was it. They thought he was a Campriano, that he could help their enslaved friends. He shook his head and Anwar's horn jabbed at him, driving Dominique to his knees.

"Wait!"

The other two leranons nodded knowingly. "He going to work with us," the big one said.

Behind him, Dominique felt the yawning space of the deep chasm. If he fell over the edge, nobody would ever find him, just like Tibor in the stories.

"I would like to help you. I would. But I am not a Campriano. I've never been to Carnillo."

Dominique felt a warm puff on his hands as Anwar let out his breath with a derisive snort.

"I'm an Estorian," Dominique went on, speaking more quickly now. Maybe if he could explain, they would let him go. "I've been banished. I'm going to the mountains to . . . to . . . I'm not sure, actually. To hear something, I think."

"Quiet!" Anwar spoke sharply but he backed off just far enough that Dominique no longer had to lean backwards.

"Estorians don't capture leranons," Dominique blurted out, deciding not to add that his people were terrified of the great winged beasts.

"This is true," the big leranon said. "Not so many Estorians come over the River Epilobium."

The third leranon spoke. "What is your name?" he asked.

"Dominique. Dominique Elnedo."

Anwar thrust his horn up under Dominique's chin and Dominique tilted his head up with a cry of terror.

"Elnedo," said Anwar, "is Campriano name."

"No!" Dominique shouted. "I am an Estorian. I came across the river, past Lagrace—"

"Wait," the big leranon said. "Sniff again, Cornelius."

The third leranon pushed his nose into Dominique's side. Dominique's breath came in quick, short gasps as Cornelius sniffed his hair, armpits, and feet.

"Yagabono," Cornelius said with a cough. "And fear and something other." He sniffed again, inhaling deeply. "Not right for Campriano."

"Because I am not a Campriano!"

The leranons put their heads together, muttering.

"Open bag," the big leranon commanded.

Cornelius took the sack, looked inside, and sniffed at all the pockets.

"No weapons. No arrows for hunting."

"I tell you, I am not a Campriano. But there is a Campriano around—he has two horses. I saw him. Why don't you catch him?"

The animals conferred again.

"We take you home."

When Polento awoke, he was a prisoner in their black cave, stone walls wet with the blood of innocent victims, air filled with the cries of lost souls.

Dominique wasn't at all sure he wanted to go anywhere with the leranons, never mind to their den. Not that he had any say in the matter. If he didn't go with them, they might toss him over the edge of a cliff or spear him with one of those great horns.

"My name is BellaMinka," Dominique's mount said. "Bella. And this is Anwar, and that is Cornelius."

"We must take him back?"

"The boy is hurt, Anwar," Bella said. "And maybe he not lying. We can not hurt him." The laranon kneeled down again for Dominique.

Dominique let out a little sigh of relief as he clambered on Bella's back. "Maybe," he said, "maybe I can help you."

"Ha!" Cornelius laughed. "You small boy can do what?"

"Uhhh—" Dominique wished he hadn't said anything. "I . . . I don't know. But I am very grateful you saved me from the incubus, so if I can . . ." His vague promises sounded empty, pathetic.

"How come is your arm hurting?" Anwar asked, and Dominique gave him a grateful look for changing the subject.

"It's nothing serious," he said. "I wrenched it, is all, trying to get out of a yagabono pit." He didn't have a chance to explain further because on some

191

unseen signal, all three leranons leaped off the edge of the rock. Dominique's stomach lurched and he grabbed hold of Bella's mane.

"Where you are coming from?" Bella asked, puffing slightly.

"From the Estorian ceremonial camp in the Aspen Woods."

"You cross the river? Alone?" Anwar asked.

"We not cross river," Cornelius said.

"Good noses, better ears," Anwar said, wiggling his for effect.

Dominique laughed, shocking himself with the sudden flood of good feeling. He was alive. For the moment, at least, the leranons weren't going to kill him.

"The crazy old serpent—her music, her magic, is strong," Cornelius said, flying just above Bella and Dominique.

Bella rolled an eye back to get a better look at his passenger. "Your magic is very big?"

"No. Not really."

"He lies!"

"Be quiet, Cornelius," Anwar interrupted. "Nobody like talk of secret magics."

Bella nodded his great, noble head, making them bob up and down in the air.

"It wasn't that hard, honestly. I just closed my eyes. . . ." Dominique's voice trailed off. How could he explain how he had survived? It was just luck, really. But maybe it was a good thing the leranons thought he had some magic powers.

"Where you are going?"

Dominique smiled in the dark. At least he could answer that question easily enough.

"To Rain Mountain. To the Dancing Falls and—"

"Ahhh, the Cave of Departure," Anwar finished for him.

"You know where it is?"

Anwar nodded and snorted. "Close from our cave."

"Your cave?"

"Not far from the falls. Sometimes others go in behind there. We know the way."

Dominique nodded, relieved the cave existed and that he might actually get there. At the very least, these three might be able to give him good directions—if they didn't hold him hostage or change their minds and kill him.

"How far away is it?"

"Not far now."

In the dark it was hard to see details of the terrain below. In places, patches of snow glowed as if lit from beneath. Every so often, Dominique gently squeezed the deerskin sack, just to make sure Navina was still there.

As Bella's steady wingbeats carried them deeper into the mountains, Dominique relaxed a little until he was almost enjoying his ride.

The tusk rose directly ahead like a giant beacon, guiding the flight of the leranons.

"Are there any yagabonos up here?" Dominique asked.

Anwar answered from where he flew just to the left of Bella's wingtip.

"The ground has many rocks," he said. "They no can dig pits."

"Too lazy," Cornelius added. "Yagabono no like to carry things so far."

"Why do they collect all that stuff?"

Cornelius answered with a snort of derision. "Not very smart."

"That is not polite," Bella said, panting.

"Yes, but true."

"They are what you call scabengers," Anwar said.

"Scavengers," Dominique corrected.

"Scavengers, yes. They like to have things."

"Do they ever bother you? Attack you or anything?"

"Never!" Anwar dove beneath Bella's belly and then appeared at Dominique's other side. "We stay away from the smell."

Cornelius swished his tail, tilting in the air.

"Watch out!" Bella cried as he slid sideways through the air. Dominique clamped his knees more tightly around his mount's shoulders.

The tusk rose up out of the side of the mountain, unmistakable even in the dark.

"Hold on," Bella said. "We circle once and then go down."

24

THE HEALERS

Tara laughed, and the sun came out again.

Dominique locked his legs tightly over Bella's shoulders and braced himself for a landing. They slowed and made a steep turn in a narrow, rugged canyon. Jagged mountain peaks loomed all around them. When Dominique looked up it felt as if the mountains were tipping in on top of him. He fixed his gaze on Bella's ears and hung on.

At one end of the canyon water tumbled and roared, bouncing and splashing over boulders en route to a churning whirlpool at the base of the cliffs. As the group swooped in front of the falls, the air temperature dropped and Dominique and Bella were sprayed with a fine, cool mist.

Wet now, they soared back down the canyon. Bella reared in the air, slowing them down. Dominique threw himself forward onto the leranon's neck so he didn't fall off backwards.

"Ow!" Bella complained. "Be careful!"

"Ahhh!" Dominique screamed as the cliff face loomed directly ahead. "Watch out!"

Bella ignored his passenger's hysterical shrieks and landed nimbly on a tiny ledge with a couple of short hops. His tawny haunches tucked underneath his body and he kept his wings half spread for balance.

"You are not a good rider," Bella remarked, indicating that Dominique should dismount.

Dominique did as he was told and slid carefully to the ground, alarmed to find his legs quivery and weak. A massive boulder rose from the ledge on which Bella had so skillfully landed, and Dominique pressed his back against it, letting his knees buckle so he could sit down.

Beyond the ledge, Cornelius and Anwar continued to circle. Bella shook his wings and a shower of water droplets glistened like white jewels as they reflected a million moons. Then he folded his wings, stepped forward, and disappeared.

Dominique craned his head sideways but could not see exactly where the leranon had gone. Cornelius, and then Anwar, repeated Bella's nimble landing on the narrow stone ledge. Each shook the water from his wings, folded them, and then stepped into the deeper shadows around the end of the boulder.

When the tip of Anwar's long tail slipped from view, Dominique stood up on still-wobbly legs. Using one hand to steady himself against the sheer rock face, he slowly felt his way toward the boulder, so large it seemed like a cliff itself. Each time he put any weight on his left leg, pains shot from his ankle to his knee. He sucked in his breath and held it as he hobbled forward.

Though he strained to hear the voices of the leranons, the relentless roar of the falls filled his ears and he had to fight away a swell of panic as he crept along.

As far as he could tell, there was no way on or off the ledge, except for flying. What if the leranons had jumped off into the shadows and left him there? What if they had only pretended to believe him when he said he was an Estorian? What if they really believed he was a Campriano labour-trader and had abandoned him to the vultures as an act of vicious revenge?

Dominique had nearly convinced himself he was doomed when he heard Bella's voice close by. "Are you coming in?"

"In wh-where?" Dominique sputtered. "Where are you?"

Bella's horn and then his head appeared from behind the boulder and Dominique then saw that there was a tall, narrow opening in the cliff face, concealed by the boulder and hidden in shadow.

Dominique stepped into the chill darkness of a long cave only just wide enough for the leranon to back up. Dominique could touch both walls when he extended his arms out sideways. His fingertips felt moisture trickling down the walls and he pulled his hands back.

And the walls were bathed with the blood of their victims.

After a sharp bend, the small amount of light seeping in from the entrance was completely blocked off. Dominique felt his way around another corner and then another, following the crunching sound of Bella's hooves on the stony ground.

"Wait," he whispered when Bella got too far ahead. He blinked in the total darkness, slowing down as he grew less and less sure of himself.

"Not long now," the leranon said. "Come on."

Dominique stepped around another bend and emerged into a cavernous room lit by a dozen flickering torches set into cracks and crevices in the cave walls. Though some of the rock walls glistened with moisture, the dribbles did not look red.

About a dozen broad platforms had been carved into the rock around the room and on each of these stood, sat, or lay a leranon or two. It was a whole flock of leranons. Or a herd—Dominique wasn't sure. "English, please—for our guest," Bella announced.

"Papa! Who comes?" a young leranon said with an excited squeal. Unlike the flowing manes of the mature animals, the youngster's was short, fuzzy, and cream-coloured.

"Wings down inside," Bella warned with a growl. The youngster folded her wings obediently, though there was no way she could keep still.

"Kyrie. Sit down, please. Remember your manners."

Kyrie crouched, her eyes sparkling, her gaze never leaving Dominique's face. Her tail twitched back and forth, back and forth, though she said nothing more.

"We found hurt traveller," Bella said. "An Estorian." Dominique noticed how all the other leranons leaned forward and pricked their ears in BellaMinka's direction. Dominique wondered if the big leranon was some kind of king.

"Who's that?" At first, Dominique didn't understand Kyrie's question. Hadn't he just been introduced? Then he noticed his bird struggling to get out of the deerskin sack.

"Navina!" Her head poked out, but the rest of her body remained trapped inside. "Wait—let me untie this."

The moment she was free, she crawled up the outside of his tunic until she reached his shoulder.

"She's my bird, Navina."

"Mama! Kasyapa!"

The leranons whispered to each other as they stared openly at the kasyapa bird, who preened her tail feathers as if it were completely normal to visit leranon caves in the middle of the night.

"Charla?" BellaMinka spoke with such authority Dominique felt sure he must be the leader. "Charla, can you help this boy?"

A graceful leranon stepped forward. She had a flaxen mane and haunches of a much darker brown than BellaMinka's.

"Show me," she said simply. Dominique had never heard such a beautiful voice. All around, the eyes of the leranons watched Dominique's every move. He moved towards Charla and held out first his arm, then his ankle.

The wrist was swollen and misshapen. An angry red gash encircled his arm where the rope had bitten into his flesh.

Charla's warm, moist breath puffed softly against the injury.

"Move your fingers?"

They were stiff, but Dominique could, indeed, move them a little.

"Come."

Charla turned and walked towards a pool in the middle of the cave.

"Kyrie? Will you help?"

"Oh, yes!" The young leranon leaped to her feet and in two lively bounces was right beside Charla. Though she kept looking away whenever he looked directly at her, out of the corner of his eye, Dominique could see her staring. The leranons probably didn't have many visitors.

"The dipper, Kyrie."

Kyrie made her way around the edge of the pool to where a long-handled wooden dipper lay on a smooth slab of stone. She dipped it into the water with her mouth. Being very careful not to spill any, she retraced her steps until she stood at Charla's side.

"Thank you," Charla said. Then, to Dominique, she added, "Give your arm."

Dominique did as he was told. Charla took the dipper from Kyrie, who rocked back on her haunches to watch. Charla tipped the dipper so a few droplets dribbled onto Dominique's arm.

Where each drop fell, Dominique felt a tingle— a slow, icy-burning sensation.

"This goes good, neh?" Kyrie asked.

Dominique nodded. It was as if a golden light bathed his wounds.

"The honey-gold is good, yes?"

Charla nodded ever so slightly, agreeing with Kyrie. Then she tipped the dipper again so more droplets fell on the bruised and swollen skin.

"Turn it," Kyrie instructed. Dominique looked to Charla's eyes and found approval. He turned his arm. It seemed a little less stiff already.

"Hold still. Think of honey-gold more," Kyrie instructed. With a job to do, she was much calmer. Her dark eyes followed Charla's movements as the older leranon continued to sprinkle the healing water over Dominique's arm. With the dipper held between her teeth, Charla couldn't speak.

The treatment lasted several more minutes. The two leranons repeated the procedure for the ragged bites and scratches on his ankle where the incubus had grabbed hold of him. When the dipper was empty, Charla gave it back to Kyrie, who returned it to its place on the smooth slab.

"Thank you, Kyrie." Charla added something in Leranese.

The young leranon ruffled her wings in protest. Looking over her shoulder as she went, she returned to where Dominique had first seen her—on a wide ledge with two other youngsters. They, too, had fuzzy manes.

Dominique inspected his arm. The skin looked different—pink and fresh, no longer raw and swollen.

"A scar will come," Charla said. "I cannot stop that."

"Thank you," Dominique said. "Thank you very

much." He wished he had something he could give the kind healer.

Seeming to sense his desire to pay, she lowered her head and said, "Bella say you are Estorian?"

Dominique nodded, glad he wouldn't have to explain, again, that he wasn't a Campriano.

"You can say a story for us. Yes?"

Kyrie's exuberant bouncing up and down and mad swishing of her tail brought a sharp "Kyrie—be still!" from Bella.

"I . . . I . . . I don't . . ."

Bella interrupted him. "You are hungry? And tired. Rest first—then you can tell for us."

Dominique looked from Bella to Kyrie to Charla. He could hardly say no, not after everything they had done for him. Reluctantly, he nodded.

"Very good!" Charla said. "BellaMinka is right. Must you now rest. There is not so much left from the night."

After eating his fill of starchy tappa roots, he sank gratefully into the soft piles of dried grass the leranons had spread on a narrow ledge towards the back of the cavern.

Anwar moved from smoky flame to smoky flame, extinguishing each with a long-handled ladle similar to the one that Charla had used to treat Dominique's arm.

"Find somewhere to sleep," Dominique said, gently tossing Navina upwards before the last light blinked out. The bird settled on an outcropping of quartz not far from Dominique. The cave plunged into darkness so black Dominique couldn't see his fingers even when he wiggled them right in front of his face. He had never been anywhere so totally dark.

"Hoh, Mama? Estoriano . . ."

"Shhh . . ."

He could imagine what Kyrie was whispering. She was looking forward to his story, no doubt about that. Dominique turned onto his side, reached his hand out to feel for the rock face beside him. What story could he tell? He rolled back in the other direction, careful not to fall off the edge of his sleeping platform.

What would happen if he couldn't think of anything? Would the leranons cast him out? Where was he, anyway?

He would stay awake until he thought of a story.

Once there was a boy called Tibor. . . . That wouldn't work. Tibor had some trouble with leranons. So far, anyway, these leranons were treating Dominique quite well. There was no need to antagonize them.

When Tara danced, her arms lifted high. . . .

No. Tara stories were out of the question. The leranons might know a boy couldn't tell women's stories.

Dominique squeezed his eyes shut, concentrating. The sighs and deep breathing of leranons settling into sleep filled the space of the cave. One of them shifted in deep straw bedding just beyond his feet.

I will stay awake until I think of a story.

That was his last thought until he was woken by the sizzle and pop of a fat alabaster fish cooking over the fire.

REPRIEVE

*The witch cackled. "Eat, then!" she said. "You
can't continue your journey with arms as thin
as sticks and no hair on your head!"*

With the arrival of morning, the cave was no longer
pitch dark. A high, narrow fissure extended
upwards directly above the fire, acting as a chimney
and letting some daylight into the heart of the cave.
The sides of this natural flue were black with soot.

The sunlight that did filter in wasn't enough to
illuminate all the corners of the cave, so someone
had lit the torches again. Leranons came and went
in small groups through the narrow opening
Dominique had used when he arrived the night
before.

When Kyrie and her mother returned, Kyrie
bounded straight over to Dominique.

"For your bird," she said.

Kyrie held the top edge of a leather pouch gently between her teeth. Dominique took it from her and shook the contents onto his palm: seeds, yellow festio berries, and cacabo nuts. "Hey, Navina! Breakfast!"

Navina dove down from her perch, nimbly landed on Dominique's thumb, and tucked right in, pecking hungrily at the small heap of goodies.

"When is the story?"

"Kyrie. Hush." Charla moved behind her daughter, nudging her gently. "Let the visitor eat."

A very dark leranon nodded at Dominique from where she stood by the fire. She lifted the fish, skewered on a sharpened stick, and pulled her lips back in a menacing grimace.

"Go," said Charla. "Your fish is ready."

Dominique crept across the cave and took the steaming fish. The aroma overwhelmed any last worries he might have had about the leranons wanting to poison him.

"Mmmm." Dominique drooled as he ate the fatty fish, pulling the skin away with his fingers and nibbling at the flesh with his teeth.

"Good spice?" The dark leranon smiled again and Dominique decided she didn't mean to be scary. She probably didn't realize just how big her horsey teeth seemed to a person.

Dominique nodded at the heavyset leranon, who indicated her name was Vefele.

"Perfect. Very mmmmm . . ." He licked his fingers. "Very good."

Vefele squatted back on her haunches and

studied Dominique.

"We no eat." She poked her horn towards the fish in Dominique's hands and he jerked backwards, nearly dropping his breakfast on the ground.

"Just grass?"

Dominique tried to be polite, but it was hard to have a conversation with a creature who spoke so little English. He was glad Charla, BellaMinka, and some of the others were more fluent.

"Grass. Yes, grass." She spoke slowly, as if tasting the word in her mouth.

Another group of three leranons came into the cave and one of them stared at Dominique. "Campriano-neh?" he heard the animal mutter. Dominique turned back to Vefele, who was cleaning her horn by pushing it back and forth along a shelf piled deep with moss.

"Where does everyone keep going?"

"Eat."

"No. Thank you—I've had enough." Dominique leaned back and patted his stomach.

"No. Eat." Vefele jabbed her horn in the direction of the entrance. "Grass get."

"Oh! You mean they are going outside to eat? Grazing?" Dominique mimed eating some grass and Vefele flashed her teeth at him again and returned to cleaning her horn.

"Big dangerous," Kyrie said from behind him. Dominique started—he hadn't heard her approach. She was not alone. Charla nodded a greeting.

"Campriano hunters," Kyrie said, wrinkling her upper lip. "In old times . . ."

"Me, baby," Vefele broke in.

"We go all at once for grass. . . ."

"Big many leranons . . ."

"Now go two or three—better for hiding."

Navina flew over and landed on Kyrie's back. She picked out fleas burrowing into Kyrie's soft puff of mane, trying to escape the bird's quick beak. Navina was still hungry and the fleas were delicious, crunchy, and plentiful.

Dominique wasn't quite sure he had understood Kyrie.

"You go two or three together?" He shook his head. He was beginning to speak English as badly as they did! "You mean, you always travel in small groups?"

"Yes!" Kyrie's tail flicked from side to side. "Good, better safe."

"It's safer that way? So the Campriano hunters don't get you? Or find your cave, I guess?" Dominique could imagine how hard it would be to hide a herd of fifty big leranons.

Kyrie bent her forelegs and kneeled between Vefele and Dominique. "Yes. Story now?"

"Kyrie! Don't be rude." But the way Charla looked at him, Dominique knew he couldn't delay much longer.

BellaMinka was in the next group to slip into the cave. He strode over to Dominique.

"You are ready?" He didn't wait for Dominique to answer. "Here. This place is good. The fire is good warm for listening."

Dominique stood awkwardly as the leranons

pushed closer. Not again! Another fire, another Story that wouldn't come. The ring of leranons tightened around him, their horns pointing in towards the centre of the circle, towards the fire, towards Dominique.

CHAPTER

26

THE STORY

All night the women worked, weaving their hair into strong ropes. And as they worked, they told stories.

Dominique licked his lips and his eyes flicked from one leranon to the next until his gaze met Kyrie's.

"Story good," she said, her mouth softening into a smile. Several leranons squatted until they crouched with bent knees, their bellies flat to the ground.

They crept closer still, waiting, ears twitching, tails waving slowly back and forth.

Tara rose, her long hair flowing in the spring winds.

Dominique heard his mother's voice so clearly he turned and looked behind him. His shadow yawned across the unforgiving stone. There was nothing for it. He'd have to make something up.

"This story," Dominique said, turning back to his

audience, "is about a boy who went on a long journey." He steeled himself for an attack, but the leranons didn't jump on him. Maybe they couldn't tell the story wasn't coming from Beyond. Maybe they didn't care.

Kyrie sighed and rested her chin on her mother's back.

"A long time ago, the boy left his village. He had only his shirt and . . ." Dominique stopped. What next? What else could the boy have taken with him? What kind of small object would fit in a boy's hand? Nervously, Dominique's hand found the Namingstone hanging around his neck. And then, the words came, tumbling one over the other in a torrent.

"He had only his shirt and in his hand he held a rough stone. The boy's name was Niquelo."

Dominique made his voice loud and strong when he spoke of Niquelo crossing the plains beneath a full moon. He made the sounds of the wind and rain when the storms came. He told of Niquelo fighting the river serpent, Lagrace, with his bare hands. Dominique explained how Niquelo, by touching his Namingstone, had gained magic powers.

"Niquelo threw back his head and laughed as his arms turned to wings and he flew from the deadly grasp of the evil serpent."

Dominique let loose a long, wailing cry when Niquelo slipped and fell from the side of a mountain. Kyrie buried her face in her mother's mane.

When Dominique finally finished, his voice dropped and he spoke in the quiet tones of sorrow used whenever a teller described the death of a hero. He flushed when he heard several of the leranons snorting softly in appreciation. They really didn't seem to have any idea he hadn't told a real Story. His tale hadn't come to him from some magic place Beyond. Dominique had just made it up and they hadn't noticed.

"Thank you," Bella said. "If you visit us again, we would like to hear another."

"Good story!" Kyrie sighed. "Here." She stepped forward and presented Dominique with a candle and a length of twisted dried grass. "For make light in cave," she said. "And this." Kyrie nudged a vial forward across the stone ledge towards Dominique. "Gold water. For fixing hurts."

"Thank you."

"Yes, good," Vefele said, and several of the others agreed.

Dominique didn't feel good, though. His stomach turned as he felt the weight of the gifts in his hands and realized what they meant. Not only did he not deserve them, he would be leaving soon. He looked for Navina, pushing the panic back down, burying it somewhere deep inside. The leranons backed away and slowly resumed their comings and goings. Navina dropped to his shoulder and cuddled against his neck.

"You must go," BellaMinka said. "We cannot keep you from your journey. Go now."

Navina lifted her wings away from her body but stayed on Dominique's shoulder.

"Anwar? Show the boy the way to the cave."

"Now?" He could hardly believe he was being sent away again.

"The sun is good. Your arm is good. You have come for the cave, and so, you must go."

211

27

CAMPRIANO

Elviron crashed down into the pit of stones. If only he had taken the other route, the road by the Chanmari Sea.

"See? Not so far."

Anwar nodded across the canyon. Dominique stood at the leranon's side on the ledge outside the cave. In the sunshine, the place was transformed. Far below was a rush of tumbling water, dashing away from the foot of the churning waterfall.

"The Dancing Falls," Dominique murmured, feeling a squeeze of excitement in his gut. Where the falling water splashed into a swirling pool, spray filled the air with rainbows.

"Come."

Dominique tucked Navina inside his bag. She squawked and struggled. "Shhh. It's safer in there. You can come out again later." Anwar kneeled down and Dominique scrambled up between his wings.

It took only a few seconds to leap off the ledge and swoop across to the other side of the canyon. There, Anwar landed on top of a huge boulder, much larger than Bethusela's house.

The roar of the water was so loud, Anwar had to shout to be heard.

"Be careful!" The rock was slick, so Anwar flapped his wings to keep his balance while Dominique slithered off his back.

"Thank you," Dominique said.

"Yes," Anwar said. "I tell you something."

The leranon looked around as if worried that someone might overhear. "Think now what you want from the Cave of Departure."

"Now?"

"Yes. So you know your heart before you travel on."

Dominique nodded.

"Go now, boy. Choose well."

Dominique reached up to stroke Anwar's neck.

"I go now. Farewell."

Anwar pushed up into the air and banked hard to avoid the waterfall. He flew back across the river and kept going along towards the other end of the ravine, off on a grazing mission, Dominique supposed. Before he disappeared around the bend he turned and nodded a quick goodbye.

Dominique waved after him. Inside the bag, Navina whistled.

"Shhhh. I'm going."

He turned and climbed down the back of the

boulder, feeling for cracks with his fingers and toes. The path up towards the waterfall, though narrow and strewn with rocks and small boulders, was quite easy to find. Carefully, moving from handhold to handhold, Dominique began to climb. He thought of what he wanted from the cave. Food . . . food for certain. And maybe a container for water . . . and a weapon. He thought of Riley and the dagger the knight had left behind. That would teach the stealing scoundrel, if Dominique could find the dagger with the donkey's head carved into the handle.

He scrambled up the rocky path right to the edge of the waterfall. There, two large rocks stood like sentries at either side of a small gap. Dominique squeezed through, moving sideways until he passed into a small cave right behind the waterfall. It must have been a tight squeeze for Riley and his big belly.

Dominique put his hands over his ears to block out the roar of the falls. An impenetrable curtain of water completely blocked the view of the canyon. Dominique could see nothing except a solid wall of racing foam. It crashed so close to him he could have reached out to touch it—except, of course, that even looking at the water made him dizzy. He backed away until he felt the wall of the cave, safe and solid behind him. So, he had arrived at the Dancing Falls.

He waited for something to happen. Navina was quiet now, but his bag bulged and rippled as she moved around inside. When he reached his hand into the bag to retrieve Kyrie's candle, Navina gave him a nasty nip.

"Ow!"

He pulled his hand back and dropped the candle. It rolled towards the back corner of the cave and he dropped to his hands and knees to find it.

"Stupid bird. Why did I bring you, anyway?"

He reached the back of the cave and felt along the bottom edge of the wall. Here, it was dark, and puddles of water glistened on the floor. "Ah." His fingers closed on the candle. "Ouch!" he yelped as his head hit a low overhanging rock. He dropped to his knees and rubbed the lump already growing on his head.

Kneeling where he was, he fiddled with his flint, carefully lighting the twist of grass. When a tentative flame flickered in the grass twist, he lit the wick of the candle. Holding the wavering flame before him, he inspected the corner where he now found himself. Nothing. Where was all the useful stuff that was supposed to be here? The cave didn't seem special at all.

He went back towards the curtain of water at the front of the cave. Could he be in the wrong place? Was this a leranon trick to get rid of him? With a sick feeling he realized there was no way he would be able to cross back over to the other side of the churning water to reach the leranons' home. The thunderous roar of the water was so loud he couldn't even hear his own breathing. He shivered as the fine mist settled on his bare arms.

"Don't come out," he warned the bag as he reached inside for his feather tunic. "And don't bite me!"

Navina huddled at the bottom of the sack, sulking.

Once he had pulled on his tunic he felt a little warmer. He turned around again. Nothing.

Tibor traced the sign of the cup, of the sword, of the waterfall.

Shreds of stories pushed into Dominique's muddled mind. Again he moved towards the back of the cave, his candle held high. Then he saw it, faint, and just higher than eye level—a cup, simple and stark, etched into the rock. He reached up to touch it.

Running his fingertips along the rock he felt a ridge over to the right and caught his breath. A long line formed the bottom edge of a sword. The tip of the sword pointed into a dark corner at the very back of the cave. At first it seemed there was only more rock back there, but when Dominique carefully probed the edge of the stone he found that behind the false rock face there was a passage.

On hands and knees he wiggled in. Awkwardly holding the candle out to the side, he craned his neck so he could follow several wavy lines someone had scratched into the rock. Someone else had been here before him.

Not two body lengths into the passage it changed direction sharply. Twice Dominique bumped his head on the low rock overhead until he learned to crawl forward while keeping his head lower than his shoulders. His knees ground against the solid rock, and in places his shoulders touched the side walls.

The passage ended abruptly and Dominique fell forward into another cavern, this one even larger than the leranon cave.

"In the name of Tara," he whispered. He stood,

silent, shocked, unable to move, as he looked into the wondrous space before him.

The candle flame flickered and swayed, and he realized it was completely unnecessary to hold his light before him. Twin shafts of light poured in from far above, bathing the spacious room and its contents in a light of white gold.

And in the Cave of Departure Tibor glimpsed the past, the present, and the future. All of time was suspended in one glorious golden moment.

The walls shimmered, the stone surfaces rippling even after Dominique blew out the candle. As he drew closer, he saw images—people flickering over the shiny rock, figures in battle, others dancing, some caught in endless falls from jagged peaks.

He leaned closer and heard whispers, screams, laughter, and sobbing.

Tara dropped into the dark water and her hair floated behind her like an ebony veil.

A woman drifted in a pool of water, and a jester hopped on a donkey and waved goodbye to two children.

A castle wall appeared. Though it looked as if it was massive and solid, when Dominique reached out, his hand met only the natural rock of the cave. Where his fingers brushed the surface, the image bubbled and dissolved. He pulled his hand back as if he'd been burned and waited to see if the picture would come back. It did, but now a knight scaled the castle wall.

"Watch out!" Dominique shouted as big rocks rained down on the intruder from above. The man didn't respond but fell backwards, out of sight.

Though Dominique leaned closer to try to see down below the edge of the picture, he couldn't see where the knight had gone.

Completely covering the cave walls were story pictures like this—ripples of movement, of crisis, of joy. Dominique moved from one to another, stopping to watch and listen. Wolves of the great northern ice mountains galloped in pursuit of the first tonneck to find shelter with people, the ships Tara used to evacuate the Estorians during the great flood sailed across an ocean, the small carcass of the fallen bird, Evelyn, lay on a blazing funeral pyre.

The stories were familiar and alive. Dominique leaned closer to study a boy swimming across a river. *That's me!* he realized, shocked. He watched as the water churned around the small figure, drew back when a serpent's head broke the surface of the water.

"Don't open your eyes!" Dominique shouted, his words echoing through the cavern.

The boy in the picture struggled on. As he reached the far side of the river, the picture faded.

A new series of images played across the rock wall and Dominique watched, transfixed. A man fought hand to hand against an attacker wearing a black cloak. As his assailant turned, the blood eagle symbol rippled across his back. The first man's short sword flashed and jabbed as he ducked blows and fended off the assault. Dominique leaned closer and studied the man's face. Though the figure had the body of a man, the face belonged to a boy. Dominique gasped and recoiled in horror.

That's also me.

Dominique moved back along the walls, studying them intently. He started again as he noticed his face—with an old body. He recoiled from the vision of the withered figure and tore his gaze away. But his eyes kept returning to the horrific images on the wall. Blood spurted from a wound. . . . a prisoner languished in a dark tower. Dominique clapped his hands over his eyes and wailed, "Stop!"

The strange sounds echoing through the chamber changed, shifted, and then grew louder. He thought he heard a baby crying. When Dominique opened his eyes again a fresh image had appeared, one that made his heart constrict with longing. There was his mother, her long braids brushing across a tiny bundle she cradled in her arms, tears streaking her lovely face. Of course, he could not remember that day, but he knew without a doubt exactly what he was seeing. *Me—at the Naming Ceremony.* He whimpered.

I must leave this place, he thought and forced himself to move away. He wished he could turn and leave the cave, but his feet stopped of their own accord, rooting him to the spot in front of another picture. He watched himself crossing a bridge leading to a great walled city. Where was he? He was beside someone who wore a blood eagle cloak.

That can't be me! he thought. And yet, it had to be. In the picture, the boy wore a feather tunic, and on his shoulder, a kasyapa bird raised her wings.

"Did you take what you needed?"

Dominique spun around to see who had spoken.

"It's an amazing place, isn't it?"

The girl was a little taller than he was and dressed

in a smart leather tunic. She wore leggings, like a man, and slung over her shoulder was a bow and quiver. A tumble of blond hair was twisted into a thick braid.

"This time I took a dagger."

She held the weapon out to show him.

"That's mine!" he said, seeing the carving of the donkey's head.

She shook her head. "Not possible. Anyway, there are plenty of others."

He turned back to the wall. The pictures were gone and there was no sound in the cave now except for the girl's breathing and a faint trickle of water somewhere off to his left. All along the base of the wall was a row of daggers and knives, their blades winking in the strange shafts of sunlight.

Had he not noticed them before? Or had they appeared when he turned his back?

He bent down to touch one, expecting it to disappear the way the pictures had. But the short dagger he picked up was real. He held it, felt its weight in his hand, and turned back to face the girl.

"Don't point that at me. It's rude. Who are you, anyway?" She looked at his ankle bracelet. "Are you also here because of Lord Emberto?"

"Uhhh . . ." Where had the pictures gone? Who was this girl? She, too, wore a heavy wooden ring around her ankle. His might have been an exact copy. Dominique's mouth opened but snapped shut again just as quickly.

"Never mind the secrecy. Why else would you be here?"

Dominique stared at the sharp dagger in his

hand. For a crazy moment he wanted to stab the girl, to make her go away so he could see the pictures again.

"Have you already taken food? Rice?"

How could he not have noticed before? All around the cave, barrels and bins stood stacked nearly to the high ceiling. Sacks and heaps of goods covered the floor. Racks of weapons, bundles of shields, and strings of fresh produce dangled from overhanging ledges. The ledges themselves were covered with smaller objects—candles, helmets, and bowls. There was nothing, absolutely nothing, to be seen on the cave walls.

"I was about to get rice," Dominique said dumbly, moving to scoop some from a burlap sack.

He could not understand this place, could not understand who this girl was, why she was here.

"Funny, I don't think I've ever seen you at the palace. I thought I knew everyone. What is your name?"

A swell of rebellion rose in Dominique's breast. For days now, each time someone had asked his name he had been accused of being a Campriano. He would not give this girl the satisfaction of tormenting him again. He looked straight into her brown eyes and said, "My name is Dominique. . . ." What was the strongest name he knew? What name would make this stupid girl pay attention? The name of one of the greatest clan leaders in all Estorian history, that would do. "Dominique Bertolescu."

The girl gasped as if she had been punched in the stomach.

28

THE CAVE OF DEPARTURE

*"I will protect you," Tara said, "if you listen
closely and do as I say."*

"Bertolescu? An Estorian?"

Dominique tried not to smile. The effect of the Protector's borrowed name was far more dramatic than he could have hoped. The girl's face turned bright red.

"Cursed son of dogs!" The girl spat at his feet.

"Hey! What . . ."

The girl paid no attention whatsoever to his feeble protest. She hurled insults at him as if she might beat him to the ground with her words.

"Swine-kissing ass of rat!"

Dominique choked. He had never heard such words, especially from a girl.

"Master of deceit! Keeper of lies!"

"Hey! Put that down!"

She cut through the air between them with the tip of her dagger.

"What are you doing here?" She wasn't smiling now. She lunged forward, weapon first.

Dominique scuttled backwards, sending a stack of cooking pots clattering across the ground. He jabbed his own blade in her general direction.

"What am I doing here? What are you doing here? Who are you?"

"Why should I answer you, you creeping wad of slime!"

"Shut up!"

"Why should I? The Estorians aren't supposed to come here. This is our cave!"

"That's stupid! This is not your cave. You're stupid! Who are your people, anyway?"

The girl lowered her dagger and stared at Dominique, her eyes blazing. "Surely you have heard of the great Elnedo family?"

Dominique was so stunned, his sharp retort withered before it fully formed on his tongue.

"I see you have heard of us. Who hasn't? We are great even among the great Camprianos."

Dominique's mouth worked, but only a strange raspy gasp came out.

"My name is Amana. Amana Elnedo."

She lifted her chin and met his gaze of open astonishment with one of pure disdain.

"I should feel sorry for you. You are hardly worth the effort it would take to finish you off. You are nothing more than a liar, just like all the other Estorians. Look at you—wearing a Campriano name

223

ring. As if that would fool anyone! Take it off."

She sheathed her dagger and held out her hand.

"Why should I? I found it. It's mine."

"You probably stole it." Her eyes narrowed. "Very well. Wear it for now. It will make things easier when we cross into Carnillo County."

The girl turned to pick up a sack and Dominique saw the blood eagle crest across the back of her cloak. Carnillo County? What made her think he'd go anywhere with her?

The girl moved from one pile of booty to another. She didn't seem to hear the cries of falling knights or see the pictures of Lagrace and the river crossing. Dominique risked another glance at the stone walls. Nothing. But the images of the city, the bridge, and the travelling companion with the cloak were vivid in Dominique's mind. He looked back at the wall. Just fishing nets and rows of silver goblets. He took one of these from a ledge.

"What are you doing?"

"A gift," he said. Wasn't the name of the troublemaker Riley had mentioned the same as this person the girl knew? "For Lord Emberto."

She squinted at him. "How so?"

"I am on my way to pay my respects to Lord Emberto, the greatest man in Carnillo," he said.

"How will you find him? His palace is well guarded."

"Someone might show me the way."

"Why would anyone want to . . ." The girl paused and Dominique watched as her expression changed. "Yes," she said after a moment. "You might be useful to us." She flipped her braid over her shoulder and chewed thoughtfully on her bottom lip. "Yes. I could take you."

A strange look passed over her face. "I suppose we can go now," she said. "It seems I have found what I came for after all."

"What was that?" Dominique asked.

"You. The Lord of Grenille will have to wait."

"Grenille?" His father had gone there. A horrible thought flashed into Dominique's mind. Maybe his father would never return. Maybe he had met a nasty Campriano. Maybe he had been captured or even . . . killed. Dominique shook his head. Not possible—he must not think such things.

Amana dropped her sack on the ground and shifted her bow and quiver. Dominique forced himself to speak to the girl. If she knew of someone who had been to Grenille, maybe she could help him find out what had happened to his father.

"What's that?" Dominique asked, pointing at the closely woven quiver. "Where did you get that?"

"My mother. Where else?"

"Your mother made you a story stick?"

"Oh. The stick. I thought you meant the arrows. My father made this for me."

She reached behind her and pulled out a story stick from where it was nestled among her arrows. Elegant, with a smooth finish and decorated with brightly coloured figures, the stick was as beautiful as any Dominique had ever seen. A double string of black and red beads dangled from one end.

Dominique blinked hard, tears stinging. If his

father had come home long enough, he would have made a stick like that for Dominique. Unless . . . unless he really was dead. That would certainly explain why . . . Dominique coughed. *Do not think of it and it shall not be so.*

Amana pushed the stick back among the arrows and gathered up her sack, two cooking pots, and a small, lidded basket of rice.

"Hurry up. We must go."

Dominique scooped rice and beans into two smaller bags and eased these into his sack, careful not to squash Navina. He rolled a small knife, some cord, fishing line and needles into a blanket. He buckled a sheath around his waist and slid his new dagger home.

"Are you ready? It is getting late."

Amana plunged into the passageway leading back to the antechamber behind the waterfall. Dominique paused for just a moment, looking back into the cavern. His breath caught in his chest. The walls were alive once again with the whispers of stories. They *were* real. But only to him.

Directly in front of him the two figures stood on the bridge. As he watched, waiting to see what they would do, the light dimmed as if a cloud had obscured the sun.

"No!" he cried as the image wavered and faded. He blinked, and when he looked again, the walls were still.

"Are you stuck in there? What are you doing?"

Dominique crouched low and wiggled his way back through the narrow passage. When he reached the cavern behind the falls he caught Amana's arm and turned her around.

"What did you mean when you said you found me in the cave?" He thought, for a moment, that she had seen the image of them together on the cave wall.

"Nothing. Never mind." They both looked at the falling water before them. The cave seemed much darker than when Dominique had arrived earlier. How long had he been inside?

"It really is getting late. Do you know about incubus?" she asked.

"Of course I do."

"And leranons? They'll kill us, too, if they see us. Unless, of course, I see one first."

She fingered her bow and Dominique fought to keep his face calm, neutral.

"Why don't we stay here and leave first thing tomorrow?" he suggested.

She pursed her lips. "I'll never get the horses inside. But I could tether them more securely. You can help me gather grass, and I have grain in the panniers. We could leave at dawn." She made it sound like her idea.

"Fine. I could get the grass while you cook?" he suggested hopefully, his growling stomach temporarily overriding his dislike of the girl.

"Hah! You think because I'm a girl I will cook for you?"

"Well . . ."

"Understand this." Amana lunged towards him with her dagger. "As of this moment, you are my prisoner. You can cook for both of us."

"Prisoner?"

Dominique threw his arm up to protect his face and flung himself backwards. He thudded to the ground and cried out as a sharp rock jabbed into his side.

"Don't!" The tip of her blade touched the end of his nose.

"What a shame I can't kill you."

She pulled the dagger back and watched him as he sat up and rubbed his bruised side.

"I would finish you off now except . . ."

Dominique swallowed hard as Amana scrutinized him.

"Except . . . I had a vision. A dream where . . ."

She faltered, and with a queasy feeling in the pit of his stomach, Dominique added, "Where we stood on a bridge leading to a walled city . . ."

Her eyes met his. "The city of Carnillo."

"Hey!" The dagger tip pricked at his throat. This girl was crazy!

"You're not the boy. You are lying."

"What do you mean? We saw the same thing!"

"No, we didn't." Her lips curled slowly. "The boy in my vision had a kasyapa bird on his shoulder. Not just anybody has one of those—especially not a runt-weasel like you."

"Navina." Dominique reached to undo the sack at his side, and Amana jabbed the dagger into his shoulder, drawing blood.

"Drop that bag!"

He let the sack fall, clutching his bleeding wound, and they both watched as Navina crawled out of the bag, shook herself, and flew to sit on Dominique's head.

"I thought you were going for your weapon," Amana said, sheathing her own dagger and staring at the bird. "It's unbelievable. I've never seen a real one before. Just a painting at the palace . . ."

She reached out to touch Navina.

"Ouch!" Her finger flew to her mouth. Dominique didn't dare smile. He knew very well how hard Navina could bite. This crazy girl was just as likely to run him through as to see the humour in the situation.

Amana flicked her finger as if to shake the sting out of it and then she leaned over Dominique to inspect the tear in his tunic and the wound beneath.

"A scratch. I didn't poke that hard. I wish I had something to put on there. I'll have to go back into—"

"Wait. Try this."

Dominique fished the vial of golden water from his bag. Amana sniffed it, raised her eyebrows, and then sprinkled a few drops on the wound. Dominique tore a strip from the bottom edge of Bethusela's shift and pressed it hard against the cut, imagining warm, golden light flooding into the wound.

"Does that feel any better?" Amana asked, still staring at Navina with a mix of fascination and wariness.

"I'll be fine. It's very strong stuff. I got it from . . . from a herbalist, a healer I met on the way here."

He lifted the cotton strip away. The bleeding

had virtually stopped.

"Good. The horses must be fed." She shifted her quiver so it hung close to her side, swept the black cloak from the rock where she had left it, whirled the heavy garment over her head with a flourish, and then let it settle over her shoulders. "Then, you can cook us dinner."

Dominique's mouth fell open. She was treating him like a cicefyrian-wench.

The girl glared at him and then added, "Prisoner." The tip of her dagger protruded from beneath the cloak, challenging him to disagree.

Prisoner? No. That was not what he had seen on the wall. He and Amana had approached Carnillo side by side—as equals.

"Do not make me wait. We have much work to do before darkness falls." She turned on her heel, her cloak flaring as she went. The bright red eagle crest disappeared into the passage leading outside.

Dominique pressed the heels of his hands into his eyes and sat very still, trying to make sense of the confusion in his head. This girl couldn't just decide to take him prisoner, could she?

Navina hopped off Dominique's shoulder and darted towards the cave entrance.

"Come back!"

She whirled in the air and returned to his shoulder and Dominique shook his head. What now? Where would they go next? They had reached the cave, yes—but what about the answers he sought? They could hardly return to his people— not yet. He still didn't have a Story.

He tried to remember what Bethusela had said about journeys beginning at the Cave of Departure.

"Well, we are not going back across that river," Dominique said to Navina once he was sure the girl was out of earshot. The bird ruffled her feathers and contentedly ground her beak. "And the picture was clear as anything—you and I on the bridge outside the city walls. What other journey could it be?" Dominique nodded sharply.

Carnillo seemed to be his destination. Did it matter that this bad-tempered, misguided girl was the one who knew the way? She also had two horses—he had none. She might know something more about the Lord of Grenille or perhaps even the whereabouts of his father.

He touched the handle of his dagger and stood to follow the Campriano girl who shared both his vision and his name.

But, prisoner? The word irritated him like a splinter driven under his skin. He thought of a story.

Alessindro hid inside the grain sack and made himself very still. Even prisoners have to eat.

"Hurry up! Why are you so slow?"

Dominique looked in the direction of her voice. In the story, Alessindro had infiltrated the island prison of Hesta by crawling into an empty grain sack.

"I'm coming. I was . . . I was putting more healing water on my shoulder."

"It is nearly dark out here."

Inside the cave, too, the light was fading quickly. Perhaps he could pretend to be her prisoner.

Then he could explain to her Protector that he was simply on a journey, too. They had no reason to hold him. At least he would be in Carnillo where he might be able to learn something of his father. And maybe, it suddenly occurred to him, he could find a way to help the leranons.

Dominique stood. "Stay close by, Navina."

Navina fluffed up her feathers as he entered the passage. Half-formed plans whirled through his head. Could he trick her into liking him—the way Tish fooled the King of Saracee? He paused a moment, suddenly afraid and uncertain. What on earth could he do to make her like him? It was silly. Unless . . .

A tiny grin tugged at the corners of his mouth. *Everyone likes to hear a story*, he thought. What if he told her pretend stories, like he did with the leranons? Dominique wondered what kinds of stories she might have heard from her own people. Camprianos did not hear Stories from Beyond, he reasoned, so she would hardly expect to hear Truth. Still, he would have to make the story interesting and exciting or she would never bother to listen. He thought of Kyrie's wide eyes and the gasps of the other leranons when he had described Niquelo's fall from the cliff.

Dominique thought of the pictures he had seen in the second cave. He would tell her of things he almost knew. That would surely be as good as the lies she had always been told.

Navina's crest feathers blazed as boy and bird emerged into the last moments of the afternoon sun. Dominique spotted the horses tethered to a scrubby tree a little way down the path. Amana moved between them, speaking softly.

Dominique touched his shoulder and winced, more for show than because of any pain. The golden water was very powerful medicine, indeed. He glanced quickly across the gorge to the place where the leranons lived. The ledge was easy enough to see, but the cave opening itself was invisible from where he stood. With any luck no leranons would come or go while Amana was outside. The quicker he helped get the horses settled and Amana back into the cave for the night, the better.

"Hurry up!" she shouted, waving her arm at him.

"Yes, yes," Dominique answered. "I'll be right there."

With a final look across the churning water, he left the rocky path to search for grass. As he picked his way towards a promising clump, he began to plan how he would begin his first tale later that evening.

Once, long ago, there lived a boy called Simboni whose only companion in the world was a small, colourful bird called . . . called Anivan.

Book II
The Estorian Chronicles

THE BATTLE FOR CARNILLO

The journey to Carnillo is plagued with
unexpected dangers, but the real trouble starts
when Dominique is captured and held prisoner in
the Tower of Carnillo. Will Dominique be able to
escape? What is the truth behind the stories about
his father? Who can he trust in the land of the
Camprianos? It will take all Dominique's wit,
courage, and determination to survive
the battle for Carnillo.

www.estorianchronicles.com

ABOUT THE AUTHOR

Nikki Tate lives in Victoria, British Columbia and is a much sought after workshop leader who is entertaining, inspiring and informative. She enjoys working with young aspiring writers and has spoken to thousands of school children across Canada about the writing process. All of Tate's novels have received consistently positive reviews and have appeared on the BC Bestseller list time and time again.

Tarragon Island

Heather Blake can't believe her bad luck when her family moves from Toronto to tiny Tarragon Island on the West Coast. What will she, a budding author, write about on this rock in the middle of nowhere? How is she supposed to live without her friends in the writing group and her favourite bookshop with famous visiting authors? Unfortunately, Heather's mother is too busy getting established as the local veterinarian and her father too obsessed with his new sailboat for either of them to pay much attention to her predicament. But with a writer's creativity, Heather finds herself planning a brilliant escape—just like the Count of Monte Cristo.

Set against the backdrop of British Columbia's scenic Gulf Islands, Tarragon Island explores the outer and inner landscapes of a young girl struggling to come to terms with the imperfections of her family and herself.

No Cafés In Narnia

Adjusting to her family's move from Toronto to tiny Tarragon Island has been difficult for aspiring writer Heather Blake. Thirteen-year-old Heather joins a creative writing class but instead of making friends and working on her novel about poverty and despair, she becomes embroiled in a real-life crime investigation! Meanwhile, she finds herself in competition with an arrogant mystery writer, and in the throes of puppy love.

Nikki Tate writes with verve, humour, and absolute authenticity of twelve-year-old Heather's life-in-transition. Nothing stays the same as Heather's understanding of her island world widens and deepens. Insightful, gentle, a pleasure to read, and wise in its portrayal of Heather's determination to become a writer.

—Marilyn Bowering

THE BESTSELLING STABLEMATES SERIES!

StableMates 1: Rebel of Dark Creek
Meet Jessa, a grade six girl from Vancouver Island, who falls in love with a pony named Rebel. Jessa must learn to juggle school, barn chores, and friendship in this story of determination and ingenuity.

StableMates 2: Team Trouble at Dark Creek
Two giant draft horses arrive at Dark Creek Stables, and Jessa's pony, Rebel, finds himself out in the cold during the worst blizzard of the century. To complicate matters, Jessa and her best friend, Cheryl, have an argument, and an unexpected visitor almost ruins Jessa's Christmas vacation.

StableMates 3: Jessa Be Nimble, Rebel Be Quick
As an eventing clinic draws closer, Jessa needs to find a way to conquer her fears about water jumps. At school she's assigned to help Midori, a new student from Japan, settle in. Cheryl is no help at all—she's too busy trying to land a juicy part in a play.

StableMates 4: Sienna's Rescue

When four abused and neglected horses are seized by the Kenwood Animal Rescue Society, Jessa convinces Mrs. Bailey that Dark Creek Stables would be a perfect foster farm for one of them, but nobody is prepared for the challenges of Sienna's rehabilitation. Can Jessa and her friends save the young renegade mare from the slaughterhouse?

StableMates 5: Raven's Revenge

When Jessa wins a trip for two to horse camp, she and Cheryl are so excited they can hardly think of anything else. But Camp Singing Waters may not be a blissful getaway. Feuding campers, a lame horse and drafty cabins are bad enough, but should they have listened more carefully to Mrs. Bailey's strange comments about Dr. Rainey's experiments with witchcraft? Or, are the late-night ghost stories around the campfire just fuelling their overactive imaginations?

StableMates 6: Return to Skoki Lake

Jessa's week-long trail riding trip into the Rocky Mountains should have been the experience of a lifetime. Ignoring increasingly peculiar symptoms, Jessa sets off into the mountains, determined to enjoy herself despite feeling very ill. To her horror, she finds herself regaining consciousness in an Alberta hospital bed! This is only the beginning of a long journey of recovery, one which turns Jessa's life upside down and threatens even her desire to ride.